THE REFUGE IN TRINITY

by

Marcella DiPaolo

ISBN-13: 978-1-64395-014-3 (Kindle eBook)
ISBN-13: 978-1-64395-114-0 (Paperback)

For copyright permission requests, or for information about special discounts available for bulk purchases, sales promotions, or educational needs, write to or e-mail the publisher at one of the following addresses.

Phantasy Publishing LLC   .
35 Brooks Drive
Bethalto, IL 62010

Website: www.phantasypublishing.com
E-mail: support@phantasypublishing.com

This is a work of fiction. Names, characters, places, and incidents are either the products of the author's imagination, or they are used fictitiously. Any resemblance to actual persons, living or dead, businesses, companies, events, or locales is entirely coincidental.

Published in the United States of America

Table of Contents

CHAPTER 1

Paducah, Kentucky
February 1873

Edward Ballamy was dying. He knew it. His family knew it, and so did his enemies. They were just waiting until he was too weak to protect his family, before they came swooping in to take what they wanted. Big Ed, as he used to be called before he got so sick, had other ideas. Before he kicked the bucket, he was going to see that his family was protected and in the hands of his best friend, Rusty Simmons. He had fought with the men that now surrounded Rusty in his valley during the War Between the States. They had saved his bacon a time or two or even three, but he had repaid them many times over by doing the same for them. It was good to have someone guarding your back during a war and even in peace time.

Big Ed was married to Willamenia Peters. Willa, as she liked to be called, was quite a woman. She had stood by him when he decided to fight in the war and managed to keep body and soul together all the time he was gone. She had plowed the fields, took care of the livestock, and still managed to raise their three children.

They were carbon copies of his wife, blonde hair and brown eyes, and each and every one of them had grit. Big Ed was very proud of his little family, even if the good Lord had seen fit to give him daughters instead of sons.

Charlotte was the oldest, but he called her Charlie. She was just seventeen and in the bloom of health. She had glorious blonde hair that curled around her face and halfway down her back. She and her sisters could all plow a field, brand a cow, help give birth to a calf, milk a cow, and help put up a fence. They could shoot as well as any boy their age could and some twice their age. They had all pitched in when he had gotten sick and kept the farm from going under. He was extremely proud of his girls.

Danielle was the second daughter; he called her Dani. Dani had strawberry blonde hair that seemed even redder in the sun. She was a lot quieter than Charlie and was the calmest in the face of an emergency. He knew he could count on Dani to keep the family in plenty of meat during the course of the year. Dani was only fifteen, but already plenty of no-account cowboys and farmers had come sniffing around looking to hook up with her. Dani had shot at a few and scared away the rest. She had work to do, and she had no time for courting or whatever they called it. Thinking about kissing any of them made her want to throw up!

His youngest was Josephine, or Jo as he liked to call her. She was his wild child and had platinum white hair. Jo loved to wander the woods that surrounded his farm. She could always be counted on to know where the juiciest berries could be found. Animals seemed to trust her. She could walk right up to a rabbit or a deer and they would let her pet them. Then she would talk to them in a low voice that seemed to hypnotize them. There wasn't a horse she couldn't ride or tame. Unfortunately, Jo was only twelve. She just didn't have the muscles to do some of the harder jobs around the farm that required more strength than she had developed. But Big Ed would put her up against any male of any age in a foot race. Jo ran like a deer and didn't seem to get out of breath even after running for a long time. She was definitely his wood sprite.

He didn't like to see any flaws in his girls. And usually wouldn't give credence to their having any. But Charlie had one flaw that Big Ed would own up to. She was a little selfish and looked out for her own best interests first and then the ones of her family.

But he worried that he couldn't keep them safe much longer. A man by the name of Keifer Kutter had come to town about two years ago. Keifer was a good-looking man, but he had the coldest eyes Big Ed had ever seen. He knew what he was the first time he was introduced to him. He was a killer. Usually a hired killer to whomever paid the most money. He used the money he made to buy into businesses in Paducah. Before long he owned half the town. He ruled with an iron hand, nobody had the nerve to go against him. The Sheriff was a good buddy of his, so he wasn't any help when the decent store owners started coming to him asking him for his help in protecting their stores. The Sheriff just looked the other way and gave them a deaf ear to their stories.

Keifer didn't bother the farmers in the area too much, he knew the town depended on them for meat and produce to feed the ever-growing Paducah. Willa always said he gave her the shivers. She told Big Ed it felt like he could look beneath her clothes and always gave her shudders whenever she ran across him. When he first came, she didn't see him much. But now that the girls were older, he had gotten bolder and seemed to always be around. She would see him sitting on his horse in the pasture looking toward the house watching them do their chores. He definitely made her feel uneasy about her girls.

Charlie seemed to be pleased with the extra attention. There were always young fellers around her. She certainly knew how to flirt and loved leading the young bucks on. None of them had caught her eye until Keifer. Big Ed was damn sure that none of his girls would ever end up at the hands of that gun-slinger. He started making plans to move his family away, far, far away where he could never find them. They would start over someplace where they would be safe and where he knew they would be protected after he passed on. Rusty and the men he knew in the Yellowstone Valley in Montana Territory were men who knew the value of a good woman and had no quit in them at all in a fight. They would be just the men who would stand up to Keifer

4

Kutter and anyone else who came sniffing after his women. He just had to get them there.

Big Ed planned carefully. He didn't want to tip off Keifer that they were leaving. He just wanted to disappear one night, and no one would be the wiser. He contacted a real estate developer that had once come to his farm to buy it. He sold it for cash and all of the cattle, cows, pigs, and chickens. He loaded up his farm wagon with as much as they could carry to start over, and he had dressed his girls in jeans and flannel shirts and big hats that hid their long blonde hair. From afar, they looked just like young boys on their horses. All three of them rode their horses while Willa and he drove the wagon behind the four oxen he always used to plow their fields. They were gone before anyone knew or could stop him. He was on a mission to get his family out before anyone discovered them gone.

They caught a keelboat in Cairo to travel up the Mississippi River. It was steam powered and made good time up the currents of the River. It took them almost three weeks to get to the end of the Mississippi River and then the Missouri River. From there they traveled across land that was rich in game and had grass that grew up to touch the oxen's bellies. Big Ed had never seen such a beautiful sight, he couldn't wait to meet up with his friends sometime in March. He was tired and seemed to sleep more and more each day. He was a lot slimmer now than he had ever been in his life. He kept losing weight and food didn't seem to have the taste he had never grown tired of. He tried to make himself eat to keep up his strength and to remain hopeful for his family. But he could see their concern on their faces. They all knew it was just a matter of time, and time seemed to be running out for Big Ed.

Big Ed had sent a telegram from St. Louis to his friend Rusty Simmons in the Yellowstone Valley of the Montana Territory. It read...'Russ, we're finally on our way...stop...will arrive within three-four-weeks...stop...we have a lot to talk about...stop...Willa and the family all look forward to seeing you again...Big Ed'.

Rusty was thrilled to get the telegram. He put things into high gear to get the cabin finished for the Bellamy family. They had already put up the walls of both the cabin and the barn. Red Dalton and Sam Greer worked on the barn and a corral to put their horses or oxen in. They were also going to build stalls inside the barn.The barn was built out of sod with a wood roof. They had all lived in sod houses for several years before they had gotten log cabins built for all of them. Bo Callahan and Miller Smythe were working on the roof of the cabin, while Tate Adams and Calvin Jackson worked on putting in windows and doors. Rusty was working on installing the iron cook stove he had bought for his good friend, Eddie.

It had been years since they had seen him. They had all parted company at the end of the War Between the States. Big Ed had gone home to his family farm in Paducah, Kentucky, while the rest of the group headed

6

out west. For the last six years they had led wagon trains across the rugged western terrain to Oregon and California. During that time, they had gotten tired of sleeping outside and living out of a wagon. They had found the land in the Yellowstone by accident and had fallen in love with the beauty of the land and its bounty. Last year, had been their last one leading wagons across, but during the last wagon train, Bo had met Molly Kendrick and fallen in love, Tate had met and married Miriam Fleming and had adopted her son Mason. Miller had met and married May King and adopted her daughter April. April had died last winter after a bout with pneumonia about the same time that his son, Gus, was born. Two other families on the train, the Greer's and the Jackson's had joined them in their valley. They had all learned how to plow a field and made sure that cabins and barns were built for the Greer's and Jackson's. Babies were born right and left, May and Miller had a little boy named Gus, Ethel and Calvin had a little girl named Lizzy, and Bo and Molly had twin boys named Joe and Jake. At the present time, Vivian Greer was pregnant and so was Miriam Adams. Life couldn't get any better for the pioneers in the valley. They found peace in working together for the common good of all of them.   They fought together, played together, and worked together to forge a bond with each and every family. They were all looking forward to meeting the Bellamy's. They had all heard the stories of Big Ed during the war. They wanted to see the man behind the legend.

They hoped to finish the cabin and the barn this week. It was time to start plowing and planting. The growing time for Montana was short, and they needed to get the seeds into the ground in time for them to grow and harvest before winter again came calling. Already, the women were using the time to start getting their gardens ready. The food from the gardens fed them all year with fresh vegetables and canned vegetables from the fruits of their labor. Molly had even told Bo that they should plow a place for the Bellamy's to put in a garden. She was sure that it would need to be one of the first things they did in their new home.

Molly was a nurse. She looked after every man, woman, and child in the valley and many who just passed through. Boone, just Boone, was an old mountain man Molly had found in the woods and taken care of. She had grown very fond of the cantankerous old man. Boone wasn't happy unless he was complaining about something or someone, and Molly loved it and gave him as good as she got!

Tate Adams had been their wagon master. He had been their leader during the war and he still kept them all leading in the right direction getting everything done for everyone. Just this year, he had talked everyone into putting in a smoke house for both the Greer's and the Jackson's before they went to work on the Bellamy's cabin and barn. The two black families had come to Montana Territory last year from the wagon train and had been instrumental in teaching them all how to plow, harvest, and butcher their hogs in the fall. Both men were excellent carpenters, and their wives got along really well with the other women in the valley.

Bo Callahan was married to Molly Kendrick. Last year Molly witnessed an attempted murder. Bo's brother, Father Callahan, was a good friend to Molly in Chicago. He sent her west dressed as a nun, even had the four orphans she was finding homes for calling her Sister Ana. He had asked Bo to see to their safety until they reached Oregon. The four children were adopted before they ever got to the South Pass that split their wagon train into two groups. Sister Ana 'disappeared' and became Molly Kendrick. She and Bo had fallen in love and had Father Callahan marry them. The murderer had come after her, but the men had kept her safe. Then she and Bo became the proud parents of twin boys. Molly had the family she had always dreamed of, and Bo couldn't have been prouder of his wife and sons. They were looking forward to seeing Big Ed and his family. Molly and the other women had made them mattresses by sewing sheets together and filling them with sweet smelling grass from the valley. When they arrived, they would be able to sleep in beds for the first time in many weeks after traveling all the way from Kentucky.

Rusty was beside himself with glee to be reunited with his friends again. He and Big Ed had grown up together from the time they were knee high. They had farms that had nested close to each other in Kentucky. Rusty's parents had died about the same time that he fell in love with Willa. He and Big Ed loved the same

9

girl. She was sure something! Rusty felt like she had chosen the best man he knew to marry and didn't harbor any lingering feelings for Willa. To the best of his recollection, Big Ed had three children, all boys he thought. He couldn't remember their names, but he thought the oldest was named Charlie. When they were finishing the cabin, he had them make a really big bed for Big Ed and Willa and they also made three beds in the loft for the boys. Sam and Calvin had built a table and benches in the kitchen and even a kitchen counter with shelves for all their cooking pots and pans and dishes. The sink drained into the garden area and so did the big half barrel that sat in the corner of the cabin for baths. Rusty even had put in a pump so that Willa wouldn't have to carry water from the stream. He didn't know if they would stop in Trinity to get supplies, but if they didn't, he and Big Ed would make a trip to town the next morning to get whatever they needed to set them up. They had even remembered to plow them a patch to put in a garden. He was very proud of the work they had done, he wanted them to like their new home very much and be just as happy as they all were.

The Bellamy's finally arrived in Trinity. They stopped just to get directions to Rusty's ranch and kept on going. They were looking forward to stopping from traveling so much. Willa was worried about Ed. He had lost so much weight the last few months and his skin was taking on a yellow tinge. He didn't seem to have much strength left, and in all the years they had been together, he had always been proud of how strong he was. Willa told the girls that they only had about an hour left to go before they reached their destination. All three nodded their heads, they were tired, dusty, and very concerned about their father. Would he even live to see them at the end of their travels?

CHAPTER 2

Rusty was the first to see a wagon in the distance heading towards them. He let out a whoop and a holler and called out to Red that the Bellamy's had finally arrived. He told him to take a horse and let the rest of the valley know. Red grinned, he loved seeing Rusty so happy. All he talked about was his friend, Big Ed and all the trouble they had gotten into when they were growing up in Kentucky. He was looking forward to making some of Big Ed's children his friends. He took off on his horse to spread the news!

Rusty waved his hat beside his cabin trying to get the attention of the wagon or the riders in front of and beside the wagon. They finally waved back and veered off toward his direction. Rusty was smiling from one ear to the other. But as they got closer, he noticed that Willa was driving the wagon not Big Ed. He wouldn't be able to miss the size of Big Ed. He wasn't one of the three riders either, they were all much smaller. They certainly hadn't gotten their size from their father that was for sure.

By the time the wagon got within yelling distance, Rusty was concerned. "Where's Big Ed, Willa?"

"Oh, Rusty, it's so good to finally be here. You are a sight for sore eyes." Willa told him with tears in her eyes. "Ed is in the back of the wagon. I don't know what's wrong with him, but he's gotten so much weaker since we started on this trip. I wanted to wait until he was stronger, but he was set that we had to get out of Kentucky while we still could. He felt that if he could just get his family to you and your valley, everything would be all right. I did what he told us to do, I certainly hope that seeing you and all his friends from the war, will do him a world of good. We could certainly use some good news about now."

"Don't you worry, Willa, Bo's wife is a nurse, and a good one at that. Iffn he can be healed, then Molly will see to it." Rusty explained, "We all pitched in and built you a cabin and a barn to get you started. I even filed for a land claim in Ed's name right next to us in the valley. All you'll need is a cow and some chickens and you'll be all set. The women folk even made some mattresses out of fresh cut grass and some sheets they sewed together. They remembered all they had to do once they arrived to make the cabins a home. Whatever you need, we'll help you with it. That's what friends are for."

By now, the Bellamy wagon and riders could see the arrival of several wagons filled with women, children, and their men. They were a little overwhelmed at the number of people who seemed to be coming at them from all directions. Rusty just smiled and told them to follow him to their own cabin just over the hill a piece.

13

He and his friends would have the wagon unloaded in a jiffy, and the women could all help them put up curtains and tablecloths or whatever they do to make the cabin into a home and not a house.

Willa just nodded and drove the tired team after Rusty. She spoke into the back of the wagon to her husband, "Ed...we've arrived. Rusty and his friends have built us a cabin and put up a barn in anticipation of us arriving. There's a lot of people coming over the hills toward us. A lot more people than I ever expected...I wish you could see the beautiful land. There's grass growing everywhere I look. There's a huge wooded area as far as the eye can see. I see several streams, it's so peaceful and majestic...it kind of takes your breath away. Do you feel up to coming up and sitting beside me on the wagon seat, so that you can see it too?"

Willa could hear movement from the back of the wagon, and slowly Big Ed climbed up beside her on the seat. He smiled at each of his girls and at Willa, they had done it! This was beautiful land just like Willa had described, Ed gave a huge sigh of relief. He could die a happy man, he knew that here his family would be safe.

Rusty was shocked at the changes that had happened to Ed. He had always been a large man, tall with a huge frame. He had been as strong as an ox and the first to always see the humor in every situation. What he saw sitting on the seat beside Willa was the shell of a man he once knew. He had so many questions to ask his friends, he didn't know where to start. That's when the three boys took off their hats and their hair fell to their

14

waists! His first question would be where his boys were and who the hell were these three females?

Before Rusty could utter a question, Bo and Molly arrived with their two little boys. Molly looked over at the new arrivals and smiled. Her smile wavered as she took in the yellowish tinge that the thin man on the wagon seat wore. She also noticed how fragile he looked. Molly knew a sick man when she saw one, and Big Ed was one very sick man. She took charge.

"Bo, please take the two boys. Rusty and Red, please help Ed down from the wagon seat. Willa, why don't you go in and put down a sheet on the bed in the bedroom, we'll cover him up after I look him over. He looks like he's one very sick man." Molly paused, "Get the rest of the men and women to unload this wagon and get these poor oxen hobbled and grazing in the lush grass around the barn."

Everyone hopped to do Molly's bidding, even they could see that something wasn't quite right about the Ed they remembered and the Ed they saw sitting in the wagon. They all nodded respectful of the womenfolk who had to be Ed's children. They were a sight to behold sitting in their saddles as if they had been born there. There wasn't a homely one among them, each and every one of them were beautiful. Red kept trying to swallow and couldn't, he'd never been around such pretty girls before, he didn't even know how to act!

The oldest girl swung off her horse and the other two followed in her shadow. She walked to the cabin and opened up the door to let them carry in her father. She

15

could smell the newness of the wood. That she liked, what she didn't like was the smallness of the cabin. Why there was only one bedroom! Where would the rest of them sleep? Charlie was sure they had arrived in Hell! She would not live in a log cabin! And that's when she saw the barn...it was a soddie! It just kept getting worse and worse! How were they expected to survive out here in the wilderness with just the basic rudiments of civilization? She looked over at Dani and at Jo, Dani was smiling, and Jo was thrilled at all the woodland she could see. This would just be their cup of tea. But not hers...she wanted a frame house with several bedrooms, just like they had at home. She would prefer that she lived in town, where it was easy to go to dances and out walking with your beau, this was even worse than back in Paducah! There they were pretty close to town and it only took you fifteen to twenty minutes to get there, here it had taken them over an hour to reach the valley from town! Charlie wished she could just close her eyes and she would be whisked away to civilization, but she knew that would not happen. Now what was she supposed to do?

"Charlie...Charlie!" Dani nudged her, "Mama says we're to put up our horses and give them some grain and hobble them, so they can graze. Then we're supposed to help her in the house getting stuff put away...I'm so glad we're finally here, I didn't think we'd ever get done traveling!"

"Isn't it just too beautiful for words!" Jo gushed. "I can't wait to go exploring in the woods, I'll bet I can find all sorts of berries. I don't think we'll ever be short of game with a wood that size!"

Charlie didn't answer, she just glared at both of them and led their horses to the sod barn to put their saddles and horse blankets away. She wasn't happy, and when Charlie wasn't happy, they all knew about it.

By now they had her father in the bed and Molly was examining him. She tried to get some answers from him, but he was so tired he could hardly talk. Willa and her girls were putting away all their pots and pans and dishes. Willa smiled when she saw the pump, it would be heavenly not to have to get water from a well or even worse from a stream, especially during the winter. She remembered the first few winters after they were married, they had to draw water from the well all the time. And in the winter, it was usually frozen solid. May and Miriam had introduced themselves and their children. That's when the Greer's and Jackson's arrived. The Bellamy's weren't prepared to see black men here among so many white settlers. Charlie was the first to get over the surprise.

"Well, thank God! We'll have some servants to help us get the work done around here! I was afraid that we would be expected to do it all!" Charlie said to the group coming in the door. "We need wood chopped to get the stove going. One of you niggers get moving, don't just stand around watching us work..."

Molly was just coming out of the bedroom, "We don't have niggers here to do the work for you." She told them firmly.

"Well then, what are they here for?" Charlie argued. "If you call them by a different name, so be it. I don't care if they're niggers, coloreds, or black folks, we need some work done around here."

Molly took exception at Charlie's tone. "We call them friends, nothing more, nothing less. Sam, Violet, Calvin, and Ethel are all part of our family. You will treat them with civility, or you will answer to me!" She told her sharply.

"Me, too!" May told them sternly.

"And me, three! These are free men and women who have their own land and homes. They helped build your home and barn willingly. I won't stand by and see you call them names. Iffn you aren't civil to them, the rest of us will leave with them." Miriam told the astonished young girl.

It was Willa who hurried to soften her daughter's remarks, "I'm sorry for what my daughter implied. We're not used to living close to other families. I thank you for all the work you've done to make us feel at home. How old are your children?"

Vi spoke up first, "My older son is Henry Lee, and he's almost four. My toddler is Thomas, he's thirteen months old. We're expecting another baby in September."

Ethel's voice was softly spoken, "This is Lizzy. She's our first and Calvin and I are just spoiling her silly."

"Children should all be spoiled by loving parents." Willa told them. "Ed gave all our children nicknames when they were born. Charlotte became Charlie,

18

Danielle became Dani, and Josephine became Jo. He's so proud of his girls. He taught them all about farming. They can ride, shoot, and hammer with the best of them."

No one was at ease until a ball was rolled toward Henry Lee's feet, he picked it up and smiled and gave the ball to Thomas. Thomas broke out into a huge smile and threw the ball, and it was caught by Jo, Ed's youngest child. "Would it be all right if I take the two little boys outside and play with the ball?" Jo asked quietly.

"It would be a blessing, Jo. Thank you for asking, I'll warn you now that Thomas has more energy than all of us put together. So, when you get tired, you just bring him in to me or his daddy. We'll take over for a while!" Vi told her laughing.

Sam cleared his throat, and he gently squeezed Vi's arm, "I think Calvin and I will go outside and chop some wood. We'll need to take the chill off the house and they can use some wood for the cook stove." He nodded his head at Molly that everything was all right and then he and Calvin quickly left.

Molly needed to talk to Willa about her husband, and she didn't know if she should let her children be in the room at the same time. "Mrs. Bellamy, I would like to talk to you about your husband. Would you like to do it here, or somewhere it's more private?"

"Whatever you need to say to me can be said here in front of my daughters, we have no secrets that I know of. How is Ed?" Willa's voice trembled fearing what Molly would tell her.

"Your husband is a very sick man. Did he tell you about seeing a doctor back in Paducah?"

Willa shook her head no.

Molly took a deep breath, "The doctor told your husband that he has a cancer growing in his stomach. It's too large to operate. Right now, it's pushing on his liver, that's why he has such a yellow color to his skin. I hate to be the one to tell you this, but I really don't give your husband very long to live. A few days, maybe a week, two at the most, I really don't see him lasting much longer than that. I'm sorry to be the bearer of such bad news...I'll send Rusty for some laudanum to help ease the pain, he'll also pick up whatever you need from the store to make this place into a home for all of you..." Molly's voice faded away, letting her news sink into the entire family.

"LIAR!" shouted Charlie, and she rushed to push Molly back, "You're not even a real doctor! How dare you tell my mother such news! Dani, help me get pa back into the wagon. We'll take him to a real doctor! Now get out of my way!"

"Charlie! What's gotten into you! How dare you ever speak to a guest in our home in that manner! You and I and Dani all know that your father has been sick for a long time. This trip has been very hard on all of us, but especially your father...I believe Molly...I think I've known for quite some time that I was going to lose Ed. I just didn't want to face up to the facts." Willa told her

20

softly. "Is there anything we can do to make it easier for him?"

"The laudanum will help him sleep and take away the pain. That's about all we can do for him except morphine. I don't have any, and I don't have a license to get any. A doctor would have to administer the dosage every few hours. We just don't have access to a doctor to get it done. I'm sorry..." Molly told her even as she reached up to take one of her sons from Bo. "I promise I will do everything I can to make his passing as painless as possible." Willa nodded her head and turned around and went into the bedroom to be with her husband.

It was with apprehension that Molly took charge, "Charlie would you make a list of all the food supplies that you will need to make meals here in your own home. I'll send Rusty to town to get what you need. Be sure to put laudanum on the list and to tell Mr. McDonald at the Mercantile what it's to be used for. May would you help advise her on the amount of each item to get. We won't be going back to town any time soon with all the planting to be done around here. Also, remember to put seeds on the list. They will need seeds for their garden and for the wheat and corn that will need to be planted."

Then she turned to Tate and Miller, "Would you two begin making a chicken coup and a pig pen? When Rusty goes to town, he can buy piglets for all of us at the same time. Miriam, would you help Dani put all the supplies they have away and measure for curtains and such.   If they have some that they brought, we'll get them up right away to help the place feel more like home to everyone...Bo I need you to go to our smoke house and get some meat for the Bellamy's. I doubt that anyone will be hunting anytime soon..."

That's when Ethel and Vi spoke up, "We did bring some food with us, Molly.   Vi brought two loaves of bread that they can start using, and I brought a large pot of chili I had been fixing up for our dinner. I thought that trying to get everything put away, it would be something they could eat and be one less thing to worry about...I'll fix something else for us to eat tonight."

Charlie looked up from the table where she was making her list. She hesitated just a little bit and then she spoke softly, "Thank you both very much.   Not having to make bread and having something to eat tonight will be a Godsend." She nodded her head and continued writing what they needed.

"Charlie be sure to put down several blankets. We'll use a few of them to put around the bathing tub for privacy, and you'll use the rest to keep you all warm. Even in the spring, it gets cold at night in Montana." Molly advised, glad Charlie was capable of kindness. She sat down in the rocker to feed her two sons before she went back in to take care of Ed.

Willa knelt beside the bed, Rusty stood behind her. "Why didn't you tell me, Ed, that you went to see a doctor and how bad it was? I knew something was wrong, but I had no idea how bad it was. I feel so helpless not being able to help you..."

"Willa, love, I didn't want to worry you, but I knew we were on borrowed time...I saw Keifer meeting Charlie down in the meadow. It was only a matter of time before he made his move...and our Charlie would have ended up just like Lela Johnson...I saw her when I went to see the doctor...She's a saloon gal at the Silver Spur Saloon...As soon as Keifer was done with her, he made her one of his girls...I couldn't let that happen to Charlie...She don't believe me when I tell her what he's like...thinks he's going to marry her." Ed raised his tired eyes to Rusty. "I knew that Rusty and his friends would help you keep her away from him. I don't want to leave you or the girls...but knowing that you're here with Rusty, makes it a lot easier...Here you'll be safe and have a good life..." Ed's voice faded away as he fell asleep still holding Willa's hand.

Rusty put his hand on Willa's shoulder, "We'll take care of you and his girls. It'll be just like Ed wanted. You can be as independent as you want, but we'll see that this Keifer feller don't get his hands-on Charlie or either of the other two."

"Thank you, Rusty. This isn't what I had planned for a reunion with you and his old Army buddies. We will appreciate all the help you can give us. The girls and I are pretty good around a farm or ranch, but there are some jobs even we admit defeat to. I'm not sure that we have the muscle to break new ground for plowing."

"Don't you worry none about it. We'll see it gets done. The first year is the hardest. We'll start on the land we borrowed the sod from for your barn. It'll still

23

be rough, but much easier than trying to break ground for the first time through all the grass and roots. Even some of the men around here cussed a blue streak breaking that ground for the first time. We'll work out a schedule where we will all help you plowing for a day. It won't put us back on our own fields much, and it will get yours done too. I believe that your garden is all ready to plant. Just needs seeds and such. I'm going to take a trip into town to get whatever you need to set you up here, is there anything special you want me to get?" Rusty asked her.

"I'm sure they're making a list now, let me get you some cash to pay for all you've spent on us Rusty. Coming here to a new cabin and barn was a miracle. I thank you all for all you've done for us." Willa rose from the floor and kissed Rusty on the cheek. "You're a good friend." She walked over to the saddle pouches they had carried in with Ed and pulled out the cash they had gotten for their farm. "Take this. Take out what you've already spent on us and buy what we need...I'm going to sit here by Ed for a while."

Rusty nodded his head and left quietly.

CHAPTER 3

With all the women helping, the cabin was shaping up nicely. Miriam had found some curtains they had had back in their home in Paducah and had them up and hung in no time. Then she and Dani made up the three beds in the loft. It was the first time that Charlie even realized that they had a loft. She wouldn't be having her own room, but at least they would be sleeping in a bed instead of a pallet or sleeping bag on the ground. She increased the number of blankets they would be buying hoping they would be able to use a couple of them to shield them and give them some privacy from people in the kitchen or in front of the fireplace. Oh my God, she thought, we don't even have a parlor or a living room to entertain men who might be coming to call on her! But this time she kept her mouth shut. She had put her foot in her mouth enough times today.

With curtains up and quilts on the beds in the loft and even in her parent's bedroom, the cabin did feel more welcoming. The cook stove had been started and the chili that Ethel had brought smelled heavenly. Bo Callahan had started a fire in the fireplace and the chill was gone from the cabin. Red and Rusty had left to get everything on the list and would be back in a couple of hours. Her father was resting quietly and while he was sleeping, they finished making up his bed. He was covered with clean sheets and quilts from home. It seemed strange to see her father in bed, he was always the first one up and moving in the mornings. He usually had the cow milked and the eggs gathered before he even called up the stairs to get them moving. They all had breakfast together and then split to get whatever he had on the agenda for the day. Mama had usually kept to the house, washing, cleaning, sewing, working in the garden, and cooking. They had all helped can the vegetables from the garden and they had all helped harvest the grain from the fields. All of that was going to change with pa so sick. Charlie wasn't sure what the future held for any of them. Once the initial shock wore off about her father, Charlie accepted the inevitable. She even appreciated what these kind people were doing for virtual strangers. Because of them, her father would be able to die in a bed with his family around him. He would know that they were going to be all right, and that his friends would see to their safety. For now, that would be enough.

Rusty had a lot to think about as he rode in the wagon to town with Red. When he envisioned his friend and his family coming to their valley to live, he had never even thought that Big Ed could change so much. Rusty had seen enough of death in the war not to recognize that Ed had very little time left on this earth to live. His one wish was that his family was near Rusty and the rest of their regiment from the army. He knew that if he wasn't here, they would be to help guard them from whatever life threw at them. He had mumbled something about a Keifer or Kevin or Keith coming after Charlie. Rusty would do whatever it took to keep the bastard from his daughters or Willa.

Red was thinking about living next to such beautiful women! They were breathtaking! Each one lovelier than the next. Charlie with her golden blonde curls, Dani with her strawberry blonde hair, and even little Jo with her platinum blonde curls were enough to make you sit up and take notice. Charlie hadn't given him the time of day, Red knew he was a rancher, probably a clod hopper in her eyes, but Dani had smiled at him and even little Jo had given him a grin as she saw how gently he treated their horses as he hitched them to the wagon to go to town. He'd like to get to know Dani better. He knew she was out of his league, but it would be nice to have someone closer to his own age as a friend.

Before they knew it, they were in town and stopped in front of the Mercantile. Jonah McDonald met them at the door. It was unusual to see the men from the valley so soon after they had come in for supplies for the spring and summer.

"What brings you in so soon, Rusty?" Jonah asked them. He was a big man, easily over six feet and built like a bull. Nobody messed around in his store, he'd mop the floor with them and throw them out. He was a fair man, but he wasn't one to rile.

"My friends arrived from back home in Kentucky, they need some supplies to finish making their cabin a home. Ed, the man we served with in the Union Army, is ailing. Molly sent along a list of medicine to get for him, among them is laudanum. She said you'd have what we'd need, and to tell you, she'd only use it when necessary." Rusty told him handing him over the list that Charlie had written out.

"Well, it's plain to see you didn't write this list, I can read it plain as day!" Jonah began with a laugh.

"No, Ed's daughter Charlie...Charlotte...did the writing. Ed has three of the prettiest girls you'd ever have the pleasure of seeing. His wife is real nice, too." Rusty added as an afterthought. That's when Red saw the sign in the front window, 'Help Wanted.'

"You looking for someone to help you run this big store, Mr. McDonald?" Red asked.

"Yes, I am. I can't pay much, but I have a storage room I built a bed in and put in a wash stand. I figure that my hired help will have room and board for free and that should save me a pretty penny. The problem is, there's nobody looking for work that I'd hire! Whoever starts working here has got to be clean and good with people, I'm not about to hire some of the hobos that have come through town. They're dirty and they smell, I figure they would scare away my customers and that sure wouldn't be any good. Maybe I'll get lucky one of these days, until then give me a little time and I'll have this order filled in no time." With that Jonah started rounding up the items and putting them on his counter.

Rusty and Red headed over to the livery to see if they could buy the Bellamy's some chickens, a cow, and enough piglets for the entire valley. They were in luck, Whit James the livery owner had just what they were looking for and offered to get them delivered out to the valley sometime today. He had to put the chicks and piglets in crates to get them out there and to tie the cow onto the back of the wagon. He appreciated doing business with the valley men, they always paid in cash. They picked up some small barrels they could use for troughs. They figured that they could split them and use one side for water and the other for food. They went on back to the Mercantile to see how Jonah was faring on their list.

Jonah not only had their list completed, he had it wrapped and loaded into their wagon. All they had to do was pay what was owed. Jonah bid them good day and turned to help another customer. It was going to be another long day for him. He usually had people coming into his store from seven o'clock in the morning until after eight o'clock at night, and then he still had to sweep out the store and get something for himself to eat before he went to bed and started all over the next day. He sure hoped that he would be able to hire someone soon.

Willa couldn't believe what these strangers had accomplished in a few hours. The cabin had a warm and welcoming look and smell. Curtains were up, and a table cloth covered the table. Quilts were on beds in the loft and added a bit of color to an otherwise drab brown room. She appreciated all the help the people were doing to make them feel at home. She even noticed that every single one of them had gone home and gotten some kind of meat to help stock their larder. Even now, several of the women were sewing up some of her curtains to cover the shelves under her work counter. She was glad to see that Charlie had gotten over her snit and was helping sew up the curtains. Dani and Jo were watching all the babies on the floor on one of her quilts and chasing after Henry Lee and Thomas. It looked so peaceful, yet in the next room, her husband was fighting for his life. Molly had been a Godsend. She knew just what to do to get fluids down him, so he wouldn't get too dehydrated. She had helped bathe him and put him in a clean nightshirt. She had even helped get an oilcloth under him to protect the mattress if he should start throwing up.

Ed's color had gotten a little better after he was taken from the jolting wagon and put in a nice soft bed. He had worn himself out telling her why he had pushed them so hard and why it was so important to him to get to the valley as soon as possible. He hadn't woken up yet, Molly told her that the laudanum should keep him from having too much pain, but it would also make him sleep. Willa wanted him to be able to tell the girls good bye before he slipped away from them. So many thoughts raced through her head.

"How were they going to till the soil enough to get a crop in?"

"What were they going to do to raise enough money to buy supplies for the winter?"

"They needed a cellar and a smoke house; her girls couldn't manage to plow the land and still build what they needed!"

"She couldn't keep imposing on these kind people to keep their bodies and souls together when they had so much to do on their own."

"How was she going to tell the girls that their father wouldn't be around for much longer?"

She saw how Charlie had reacted when Molly had told her Ed was dying. How would the others take it? Was she strong enough to be both mother and father to her three girls? What if Keifer Kutter showed up? Did she have the gumption to pull a trigger to chase him away? And what would keep him from taking what he wanted with no man around to stand up to him? Willa's shoulders felt incredibly weighted down with all she was thinking about. That was when they heard Rusty and Red pull up in one wagon with another wagon following him.

The men seemed to come from all directions to help unload the wagon and take the animals in the crates and tied to the back of the wagon. Willa was astonished at all Rusty had bought, yet secretly thrilled that they would have eggs, milk, and butter every day. Charlie came out and took the blankets and immediately went back in and started hammering away up in the loft. Willa had no idea what she was doing but she was glad, she wasn't causing any more turmoil. They had enough to worry about!

"Seems like a lot of supplies, doesn't it?" Rusty asked with a grin to Willa. "We don't go to town much more than once in the spring and once in the fall to get supplies. We made an extra trip this year to get the lumber and glass and stuff for the cabin. So that when we do go, we make sure we stock up. Nobody wants to run out of food or the things we need to make food. We'd all help out if that happened to one of us, but we also like to be self-sufficient. We all like to be as independent as we can, but then again, we all pitch in to get something done, like building cabins, barns, putting in cellars, and building smoke houses."

"I was going to ask you about that, Rusty, my girls and I are pretty good with a hammer and nails. We also know our way around a plow, but I wasn't sure how we were going to do it all done." Willa told him.

"I done talked to the other men. We're each going to take one day off a week and help plow your fields. We'll do that until it all gets plowed. We'll leave you and your girls to pull a log over the broken ground and break it up even more, we'll also leave you to plant the corn and the wheat. When everybody has all their crops in and their gardens, we'll show up and build you a cellar and a smoke house. Knowing Ed, I bet your girls are cracker jack shots and will be able to keep that smoke house filled for you. Iffn you need help with the planting or even pulling the log over the ground, you just have to call. We'll all come running, you'll find in this valley, we all help each other." Rusty told her knowing she was overwhelmed at everything she was facing. "I'm real glad that Ed brought you here...I'm sorry to see him so sick...But you know how I feel about you and Ed, I'll help keep your family together and safe and sound...So will the others."

A tear fell down Willa's cheek and she turned away to go back into the cabin and bedroom. She was going to spend as much time with her husband as she could before the good Lord took him from her.

Charlie was using the blankets to build a wall giving the girls some privacy in the loft. Dani saw what she was doing and jumped up to help her, Jo just grinned and continued watching over the little ones. They had enough blankets to build a wall cutting off the rest of the cabin in the loft. They also were able to connect the top of the blanket to the roof and the bottom of the blanket to the floor to split up the three beds into each having their own little alcove. It was flimsy at best, but it made Charlie better knowing she had some part of the cabin to go to when she wanted to get away from all of them.

Red used two of the blankets to section off the large bathing barrel in the corner of the room. He figured that they would like some privacy when they bathed. He did mention to Jo that if they just lift the cork in the bottom of the barrel, it would drain all the water out to where they plowed up their garden plot. The same was true of the kitchen sink. Jo was thrilled! No more carrying out bucket after bucket of water after they took a bath! They all liked being clean and traveling for the last five weeks had not always been possible. She vowed to take a hot bath as soon as their visitors left.

Each of the families in the valley were given two piglets except Molly and Bo. They were given four, two to slaughter this fall, and two to breed. Bo wanted to raise their own piglets, so they wouldn't have to buy them every spring. He figured that one litter of pigs a year should give everybody enough pork by the time they were weaned and grown over the course of a year. Bo and all the others appreciated the hams, bacon, sausage, pork chops, and pork roasts they received from the pigs. They didn't take a lot of work or food, just each day's peelings and some corn. They seemed to thrive on the cooler night air in the evenings, and the cold in the winter didn't seem to bother them too much. Bo's barn was big enough to house a couple of hogs over the winter, it certainly seemed like the perfect solution.

Jo finally tore herself away from all the babies to help with the new additions to their livestock. She loved the little piglets and laughed as Mason and Red ran after them trying to catch them and put them in their pens. She finally sat down in the yard with a handful of corn and waited for them to come to her. It seemed like it only took minutes for them to be eating corn out of her hands. She scooped them both up and gently put them in their pens. Then she turned to Red and Mason and smiled. Both boys turned bright red! Imagine being bested by a girl that wasn't even as old as they were! Bo and Miller and Tate stood there and laughed.

When it came to the chickens, they just told Jo to turn them loose. She did after she dragged their crates into the pen! Then she just opened up the lids and they seemed to fly out! Jo made sure they had water and corn meal to eat and left through the gate. The last thing she did was to stake out the cow, so she could start eating the lush grass like the tired horses and oxen they had brought with them.

After everything was put away, the families started loading up to leave for home. Everyone had animals to see to and meals to make for their hungry men and children. Willa was glad to see them leave, she needed time alone to sort out all her thoughts and to prepare her daughters about Ed's impending death. Yet, she was sorry to see them leave because they had been a protective barrier against all the thoughts that she had held at bay all day. Molly promised to come back tomorrow to check on Ed, and she promised to come as soon as she could if they needed her sooner than that. It seemed like in minutes everyone was gone, and it was just Willa, Charlie, Dani, and Jo standing at the front door and waving to everyone as they left.

They had come a long way in one day from the wagon being pulled by the tired oxen. They had come to a cabin and their friends had helped make it into a home. They had the means to plant a garden, crops, gather eggs, milk a cow for milk and butter, and they had acquired pigs, chickens, and a cow. For tonight they were satisfied.

CHAPTER 4

The next few weeks were busy ones for the men and women in the valley. Crops and gardens took precedence over everything else. While men plowed the fields, women were getting their gardens ready to plant. Babies were put on quilts and watched over while their mothers started putting in the seeds. Molly and Vi and Ethel worked together to put in all three of their gardens. Each one took a turn planting and then watching over the three babies and Thomas, Henry Lee felt grown up because he was allowed to help the ladies. Even so it took almost two weeks to get all three gardens in with everything else they were doing. Molly talked about starting to go berry picking as soon as the gardens were finished. She still checked on Ed every day and was happy to report that he was holding his own. Ed and his girls spent time every evening talking with him about what they had accomplished that day and what was on the agenda for tomorrow. He never left his bed but seemed to be more alert.

He felt so helpless just lying there while everyone did all the work for him. He was so grateful for his friends for plowing his land for his womenfolk. Plowing up virgin land is very hard work, even with experienced oxen and man-sized muscles to push it through. His women were gutsy, but he felt that it was a little more than they could comfortably do on their own. He knew how much Willa and the girls hated asking the men for any more help than they had already given, but he also knew that he was on borrowed time. But before he left this earth, he needed to know that they were firmly entrenched in the new ranch and life here in the Montana Territory.

Thanks to Molly, he felt no more pain. He was lucid most of the time, but he still slept a lot of the day away. Sleep was becoming a blessing for him. Back in Kentucky and on the way here, sleep had been hard to do with the pain constantly causing him to sometimes gasp for breath and keep from doubling over. He was comfortable in the big bed they had made for he and Willa and he never tired of looking around the well-made cabin. He was constantly amazed at how homey they had made the cabin after only a few days.

Willa and her girls had come to terms about their father. No one ever mentioned his impending death. They all acted like he would get better and start helping them around the ranch, but each one of them knew that their father would never walk out of the cabin again. They each dealt with his sickness in their own way. Charlie acted mad at everyone and was prone to lash out first and apologize second. She bossed her sisters and continually told them what to do. Dani kept everything to herself. She spent long hours in the barn caring for the animals. Jo roamed the woods and forests around their home. The feeling of freedom she felt as she walked and ran helped her cope. Jo never failed not to show up whenever there was a birth with one of the animals. She was there when Ethel's cat had kittens. She was present when Mason's dog had puppies, and when the horses foaled. She had never said anything about it, but Molly was pretty sure that Jo was also present for many of the calves being born with their cattle.

Willa held it all together for her daughters, and she didn't want Ed to feel she wouldn't be able to manage without him. She was trying to be strong for his sake and for everyone else. She knew that one day soon, there would be a day of reckoning, but heaven help her, she hoped it was a few days or even weeks ahead.

Willa and her daughters loved berry picking with the other women. That was the one time she left Ed's side, Rusty usually came and sat with him while she was gone. There was a lot of laughter and teasing as they picked berries, wild onions, and mushrooms. Molly didn't let a time go by that she didn't dig up some flowers or a flowering bush or tree. She told them all that by the time she was too old to go traipsing all through the woods, she'd have enough planted around her home to take care of them all. They all laughed, but they all helped her get her new-found treasure home.

Dani, Jo, and Willa felt at home with these women. Charlie did not. They were all content to be wives of ranchers or farmers, she had no intention of ever falling in love with a farmer or a rancher. God forbid! She couldn't imagine spending the rest of her life cooking, canning, cleaning, and washing day after day, year after year! It would drive her crazy. She wanted something more out of her life. She wanted more people in her life! Only seeing her sisters every day, maybe one of the men as they plowed their fields wasn't enough. At least not for her, anyway! She felt like she was biding her time waiting for her father to either get better or die. She wanted the fields to be in and the garden done, so that she wouldn't feel like she was letting her mother down by leaving. But she was getting out of here, she didn't know where she was going, but the call of what her future might hold for her kept her dreams alive.

Jonah McDonald had not gotten anyone to help him in his store. He was tempted to take the worthless sign down, because it wasn't doing him any good sitting in the window day after day. But like everything else, he hadn't found a minute to spare. So many farmers and ranchers were coming in to buy seed and spring and summer supplies, he didn't have enough hours in the day to go to the outhouse much less take down the sign? He was a proud but solitary man, who was used to doing things the way he wanted them done. He wasn't used to working with others. He didn't like to chit chat about the day, tell him what you wanted, and he'd get it done, but don't waste his time talking about the time of day and anything else. He had few friends. One of them was Graham Crocker, one of the Sheriff's deputies. He and Graham had been friends for many years, long before they both settled down in Trinity. They shared many memories together. They also shared a secret. A secret so terrible that if the other towns people were to hear of it, they'd probably run them out of town.

Jonah's parents had been killed when he was just a young boy. He had gone to live with his Uncle Matt. Uncle Matt owned a Mercantile in Kansas. Until the War Between the States, he had helped his uncle out running the store. He had learned all about the store frontwards and backwards, he had loved working with Matt. The war had changed everything. His uncle died during the war and left everything to Jonah. Coming back from the war, Jonah couldn't face all the memories Kansas held for him. He packed everything up and had headed north. He didn't stop until he had all his teamster wagons loaded with enough supplies to start up his own store. He was one of the first people to come to Trinity seven years ago and set up a business. Being the only store for miles around, he was able to set himself up with everything any settler, wife, or miner might need. He carried a full line of clothes, had a cellar that was deep enough to hold ice year-round and therefore fresh meat didn't go bad, he made sure his prices didn't gouge his customers, and put almost every penny back into the business. He did take out enough of the profits to build this mercantile store with four rooms for living quarters above the store. Everything was paid for and he didn't owe anyone anything. He liked that. He did get lonely sometimes, but he could live with that.

When Keifer Kutter went to the Bellamy's farm in Paducah and found it deserted and empty, he was beside himself. He was just about ready to make his move on Charlie. She was a choice piece of work to be sure and Keifer planned on her being a sure-fire money maker in one of his pleasure houses. But first he was going to have her all to himself for several weeks. He had thought he would set her up in her own house, complete with a maid and a cook. He would have access to her anytime he wanted her. When he tired of her, he'd set her up for his many customers to enjoy. It didn't matter that Charlie expected him to marry her, after he had his way with her, she'd be only too glad to do what ever he wanted her to.   He'd use drugs or physical force, whatever it took. It had worked in the past, he was sure that it would work with her, too. But now she was gone! All his time and effort wasted! He'd track her down, and when he finally found her, she would not escape again, he'd make sure of that!

He sent several of his men out searching for the direction they went, north, south, west and even east. He knew they didn't have a lot of money, so they would have had to travel by wagon. They could have gotten a ride on a train or a keel boat, but he doubted that they could afford either means of transportation. If they joined a wagon train to go out west, he might never find her. That was unacceptable!

Within a week, he had news that they were seen in Cairo getting on a keel boat going upstream. Keifer also found the man who had bought Bellamy's farm. He had paid for the farm in cash. Keifer's worst fear was that they had money to escape. He sent men to find out where they got off the keel boat and if possible where they were headed. He spared no expense. And when they found her, they were to telegraph him immediately. He didn't want her tipped off, so they could leave again, he would come and get her himself! He didn't consider her family to be of any consideration or threat to his plans. Killing her father and even her mother wouldn't bother him in the least, her two sisters would look as good as Charlie in a few more years. He'd save them for his future investment. He had been a careful man so far, he didn't see any reason why he wouldn't continue to reap the rewards of his plan.

To add to his frustration, Lela Johnson wasn't fitting into her new occupation so easily. He'd courted her, seduced her, and taken her to live in his house in town. She had a maid, a cook, a stable boy, and money to spend, but she didn't get what she wanted...a wedding ring. Even plying her with wine and drugs didn't do the trick. She hated the life she now found herself in and vowed to get out of it someway. Keifer was letting her come to terms with her new...position in town as one of the entertainers at his local saloon. She was to serve drinks and keep the customers happy...giving them whatever they asked for. Lela had other ideas. She refused to wear the clothes Keifer had made for her. She wore her long dresses, buttoned to the chin, and wearing an apron over them. Even then she was a looker! She had jet-black hair and a porcelain complexion with dark blue eyes that flashed fire when she was riled. She had a knock out figure with curves in all the right places, the men had a hard time keeping their hands to themselves. But Lela had an answer for that, too, she wore a sharp dagger in her apron. Any man that touched her, pulled back a bloody nub!

Keifer knew that he was going to have to use physical force to make her become one of the upstairs ladies who also worked in his saloon. But he could only handle one crisis at a time. As soon as he had Charlie, he'd deal with Lela one way or another...she would do what he told her to do, when he told her to do it!

Lela felt like she was in a nightmare that she couldn't wake out of. She had to escape and get as far away from Keifer Kutter as she could. She was good at sewing and often thought of opening up a milliner's store. She knew where they kept her money in the safe. Each of the girls received payment for working every night and most of the days. But they only got how much was written down in Keifer's little black book. They never received any cash, because he was afraid, they would take it and run. But that's exactly what Lela was going to do with it. She knew she was watched so that she wouldn't get some hairbrained idea into her head to get out of there. She had to plan it carefully or they would just catch her and make things worse for her. So far, she hadn't had to...service any of the men. But she knew her days were numbered, Keifer wasn't known for his patience. She'd seen the drugs they gave the girls to keep them agreeable and passive, she'd seen the drinks given to them by the bartender to keep them in a semi-drunk state. She wasn't drinking anything they gave her or fed to her. She took food out of the kitchen and ate it. The saloon cook was kind to her, she knew she was here against her will. But she'd only go so far helping her, otherwise it would be her head on the chop-block as well as Lela's.

One of Lela's many jobs was to scrub the floors after everyone had gone home after they locked up each night. She was to wash all the used glasses and clean off the tables, too. It usually took her at least two hours after everyone else had gone to bed, including the bartender. That's when Lela planned to make her move. Her clothes were already packed, tonight she would take the money that was hers and leave. She would hide in one of the many cars on the train that came through Paducah every day and every night. Where ever that train stopped at, that's where she would begin her journey. It had to be better than working here. Once she had been labeled a saloon girl, her reputation was ruined, not to mention that she had slept with Keifer.

45

What self-respecting man would want one slightly used woman for his wife? She would go to someplace far, far away and start over. She could always tell people that her husband was dead, and she was starting her life without him.

It was a busy night at the saloon, Lela felt like she had worn her poor feet down to nubs. She was tired and her back hurt from all the carrying of heavy mugs all night long. There had been a constant patter of heavy boots up and down the stairs all night. Lela couldn't even look at the upstairs girls, she knew they had to be as tired as she was and as disgusted. That's when Keifer came into the saloon. He made his way around the bar, slapping his friends on the back and giving them his phony smile. He was angry and did a terrible job of trying to hide it. She cleared off some empty glasses and took them up to the bar in the hopes of finding out what was going on. What had happened to make him that mad?

Lela soon found out it wasn't what but whom had made him so mad. Charlie's family had disappeared! Oh, thank God, Lela thought to herself. Big Ed Bellamy must have been concerned about the attention Keifer was showing to Charlie. Lela remembered that he had friends up in Montana near the Yellowstone valley.

"Moose!" Keifer told the bartender, "I'm going after her! Nobody gets away from me, not after all the time and effort I spent getting her to fall in love with me! The boys are hot on her trial and as soon as they find her, they'll telegraph me, and I'll go get the bitch. It's up to you to keep things running smoothly around here while I'm gone."

"You got it, Boss! What do you want me to do with Lela? Is it time to put her to work upstairs yet?" Moose asked Keifer.

"As soon as I get back, Moose. Things will change for hoity-toity Lela Johnson. Let things go for right now, I'm going to concentrate on getting the Bellamy girl. Between the two, the men will love them. Two beauties in the same saloon will be hard competition for any of the other saloons in the town, I'll be able to buy them for a song. Then we will really own this town! Be patient, have I ever let you down yet?" Keifer asked the burly bartender.

"Not yet, Boss. You go take care of business, I'll see to everything while you're gone." Moose and Keifer shook hands and Keifer left after giving Lela a smug look. Lela knew that her time was close to being up, she had to get out of here while the boss was gone. She would kill herself before she'd become a whore for Keifer or anyone else, and while she was at it, she'd kill him, too.

CHAPTER 5

The bar was closed. Even the bartender had left to go find his own bed, however he did take one of the upstairs girls with him to keep him company. She quickly changed into pants, a plaid shirt, a leather vest, a big bulky coat, and a stocking cap. She had rolled her quilts and blankets into a roll and had tied them onto her backpack. She quietly went into the bar from her backroom. It smelled of unwashed bodies, spilled whisky, and cigar smoke. She went into the kitchen and filled a pillow case with a loaf of bread, some apples, a chunk of cheese, a few slices of venison, and a box of matches. Then she went to the vault under the barroom counter. She knew the numbers to open it up. She had casually watched while Moose had put the money in one night while she collected all the dirty glasses and started to wash them.

'Three to the left...fifteen to the right...and twelve to the left...' Lela heard the click of the handle as she opened the door. The little black book was there, too. Lela looked how much was hers, she took it all and put it inside her pockets, it wasn't much, but at least they wouldn't be able to accuse her of robbing them. Then she saw the two loaded Colts, she grabbed one of them and a box of bullets and slipped it into her coat pocket. She might need protection on her journey and the gun would help a lot. She put her backpack on and slipped out the front door and down the alleys to the train depot. If she had timed it correctly, she should be able to get there just as the train started pulling away. She was prepared to run to catch it and jump on board. Everything went like clockwork, she was on and managed to get into an almost empty railcar. She had no idea where the train would stop, but it was headed west and that was good enough for her. She checked to make sure that she wasn't sharing the car with anyone else and finally settled down in one of the corners to catch a few hours of sleep before they pulled into their next town. For the first time in over two months, Lela breathed deeply. She was safe and out of that hell hole at last!

It took her almost two weeks traveling by railcar to reach Billings, Montana Territory. She had to warn Charlie and her family that Keifer Kutter was coming for her and what her life would be like with him. He didn't have marriage in mind for Charlie's ever after thoughts. She knew she would have to bare her soul and tell them what she had done with Keifer and her work in the saloon, but she'd do it if it could save Charlie from the anguish that Lela felt over her stupidity in falling for Keifer's sweet talk hook, line, and sinker!

She had only had to use a small part of her money for food, she had ridden in empty railcars all the way. She finally paid for a room in a small hotel. She couldn't stand to be so dirty anymore! She wanted a bath and to be able to wash out her filthy clothes. She still wore the pants and clothes she had left in. No one would be able to find her, they would be looking for a young lady not a rag-a-muffin boy.

When the boys brought the steaming water up the stairs to fill the large tub, "Don't worry about coming back for the tub tonight. I'm going to wash out my clothes after I take my bath. You can get it in the morning when I leave." Lela told them, and they nodded their heads and left.

Lela spent thirty minutes in the tub scrubbing her body and her hair clean. She wrapped herself in towels and started washing out her clothes. When they were clean, she hung them over chairs and tables, so they would be dry by the morning. She ate what was left in her pillowcase and fell into a sound sleep. As dawn was coming over the horizon, she dressed in clean, dry clothes, packed up her belongings and left out the back door. She headed to the stagecoach depot. Trinity had no train, the only way to get there was to go by stagecoach. It was Lela's understanding that the ride took about five hours. She hoped that the stage wouldn't be too crowded.

Her wish came true, only one other rider climbed aboard. It was a priest! Oh, Lord, Lela prayed, what will he do when he finds out he's sharing a stage with a woman of ill repute?!

"Good Morning!" The priest greeted her with a smile and a nod of his head.

"Uh...morning, Father..." Lela started to say, "Would you like me to ride on top?"

"Why would you think I would rather ride by myself?" The good father was very confused.

The stagecoach started up and Lela decided that she better tell the priest the truth. You just couldn't lie to a man of God! She pulled off the knit hat, "To begin with Father, I'm not a boy but a woman...And not just any woman, I'm...a woman of ill repute or at least I would have been if I had stayed back in Paducah!"

"I see..." The good father began. "Perhaps if you tell me your story, I will decide if we should be riding together..."

"That's why I pulled off the hat," Lela told him turning all different shades of red. "You just can't lie to a priest! I grew up in Paducah, Kentucky. There was this man that moved to our town. His name is Keifer Kutter, well he invested in a lot of the businesses in town, bought out a few others. He's one of the most powerful men in our town. I grew up on a farm on the eastern side of the town. Keifer started riding out on his horse and talking to me. I was kind of ignorant, I guess to think that someone that rich would ever be interested in someone like me, but I did. I really thought that Keifer was wanting to marry me..." Here Lela hesitated. Should she tell him everything? He's going to think I'm going straight to Hell for all the things I've done! But here goes nothing..." He seduced me Father and I let him, thinking that we'd be married really quick. But it wasn't to be. He took me back to town with him and took me to this real nice house with a maid and a cook and a stable boy. He kept wanting to sleep with me, and I told him we would right after he married me...He laughed, Father, right to my face. He told me he never had any intention of marrying me, he was just breaking me in to be one of the whores at his saloon!

"I was mortified and tried to leave, but he told me that if I wasn't going to sleep with him or service the other men in town, I could just start cleaning the saloon...I mean what self-serving male would want to marry a slightly used woman, right? So, I scrubbed the floors and washed the glasses and mugs every night after the saloon closed, and while it was open, I was expected to wait on the tables and serve men drinks. A couple of the men tried to get too handsy with me and I cut them with my knife that I always carry in a pocket of my aprons. Most of them left me alone after that. I heard Keifer and his bartender talking, and they were mad about one of my friends leaving Paducah after he had spent a lot of time trying to seduce her. He was going after her and bring her back. He said that when he came back, between Charlie and me, we'd have men fighting over us! He uses drugs and liquor, Father, to keep the girls in line and doing what he wants them to do. I won't do it! I ran away, but I only took the money I was owed for working there...Oh, I almost forgot, I did take some food and one of his Colts and some bullets. I figured he owed me for what he did to me. Charlie and her parents came up here to the Yellowstone Valley to meet up with some of Big Ed's friends from the war. I've got to warn them that he's coming, and he won't mind killing anyone who gets in his way.

"Once I've warned Charlie, I'll leave, and he'll never be able to find me. I disguised myself as a boy knowing it would be safer for me to travel and no one would be able to tell him in which direction I went." Lela finished and looked down to her lap. She didn't want to see the condemnation on the good father's face as he thought over all she had done. She did feel a little better getting it off her chest and talking to someone about it, but she didn't know what to say now.

"Child, you've more than paid for your sins. You have nothing to be ashamed of. Now this Keifer you spoke of, he has a lot to answer for!" Then he smiled and held out his hand, "I am Father Callahan, by the way. I, too, am headed to the Yellowstone Valley to baptize my two nephews and a few other babies that have been born since I last visited my brother and his wife. If your friend, Charlie, is there, they will know where and I'm certain that they will help you any way they can. They won't judge you. They're good people. I think maybe it's time that you quit judging yourself. God understands and has surely forgiven you."

"Do you really think so? I'd sure feel a whole lot better if I didn't think I'd go straight to hell for what's happened!" She suddenly smiled and shook Father Callahan's hand. "My name is Lela Johnson. I'm real glad that you chose this stagecoach to ride to Trinity in!" They both shared a laugh. The rest of the trip was uneventful but pleasant.

Lela learned that Father Callahan came out to Montana Territory from Chicago. Then he talked about the little parish he had become the pastor of and how he had started a little school for the children of his parish. He loved his work and was very passionate about what he had been called to do.

Father Callahan learned that Lela was a very good seamstress and hoped to open a shop in one of the little towns out west or at least work for someone who sold her designs and dresses.

Father asked her about her family. He worried they didn't know where she was or what she was doing.

Lela told him they disowned her after they saw her working in the saloon. "No daughter of mine will ever work in such a sinful place! As of today, I no longer have a daughter!" Her pa had yelled at her and her ma had cried. "I don't think they want to know what happened or where I am right now, Father. I was hoping that I could go back home after all, but it looks like I don't have a home or a family waiting for me anymore."

Father Callahan told her the story of the prodigal son and told her that someday her parents would welcome her home with open arms.

Lela smiled and let him think that, but inwardly she thought that if they didn't want her, she didn't want them either!

"Maybe after you've warned your friend, you'll find a job right here in Trinity. It's a small town but growing every day. Some day you'll look back on all this as just a bump in your life. It's going to be all right, Lela. Trust me, the Lord works in mysterious ways. He may have led you here for a special purpose." Father Callahan told her. He liked this young girl, she reminded him of Molly a little bit. Not in looks, but certainly in spunk. He thought that staying with Molly and Bo for a few days would be just the thing to start her off on her new life. He just had to hope that Lela was up to agreeing with him!

They arrived in Trinity around noon. Bo was waiting for him smiling from ear to ear! He was so happy to see his brother again, and this time under very happy circumstances.

"Thomas! It's good to see you! You look happy, your new parish must be agreeing with you! Molly is so excited, she stayed home to fix all your favorite foods to eat. Wait until you see the boys...they are sure something. I never thought that being a father would mean so much. But I'd walk through fire for Molly or my children." Bo told him grabbing him and hugging him.

"Bo! It's good to see you, too, Molly must be feeding you really well! You've put on several pounds of sheer muscle! Twin boys was unbelievable! I still can't believe that you delivered them during a tornado!" Father Callahan hugged Bo back in return. "It's been too long, that's for sure! How is everyone else in the valley?"

"Most everyone is doing real well. We're about to add several more babies and Rusty's friend from Kentucky isn't doing too well. Molly says he has a cancer in his stomach and he's just withering away right before our eyes. She doesn't expect him to live much longer." Bo continued.

"Excuse me," Lela interrupted him, "I couldn't help but hear you say that his friend from Kentucky wasn't doing very well. Would that be Big Ed Bellamy?"

"Yes, it is, and who might you be?" Bo was always suspicious about strangers.

Father Callahan stepped in to introduce Lela to Bo. "Bo, this young lady came all the way from Paducah to warn the Bellamy's of someone coming to Trinity to harm one of his daughters. Her name is Lela Johnson, and she has first hand experience of just what this character is capable of. Would you mind if she rode along with us out to the valley?"

"Course not, you know that Molly will welcome anyone who is a friend of yours. Where's your suitcase or valise?"

Father Callahan pointed out which one was his, but Lela told him, "Everything I got is in the backpack on my back and the bag in my hand. But I do thank you for the offer and the ride, Mr. Callahan." She hesitated, "I do need to tell you that...back in Paducah...I worked in a saloon. I waited tables and scrubbed floors, I didn't do any upstairs...work. I'm considered a lady of ill-repute for working in a saloon. If you have any hesitation for still giving me a ride, I understand...I'll find another way out to warn the Bellamy's." Lela's face was beet red by this time and she looked down at her scuffed boots instead of watching Bo's friendly face turn to one of condemnation.

"The ride still stands, Miss Johnson. My wife and I would love to have you stay with us for a few days if you can stand the cries of the twins and snores of Father Callahan!" Bo held out his hand, "Welcome to Trinity!"

Lela's mouth fell open as she grasped his hand. "Thank you!" Lela whispered as tears came to her eyes. If she were treated like this instead of like an outcast, she just might see if there was work for her in Trinity.

As they were loading up Lela's backpack and sack and Father Callahan's valise, Graham Crocker came into view. Graham was one of the deputies of Trinity.

Graham was a good-looking man. He was dressed in black pants, a black vest with a shiny star pinned to it, and a blue long-sleeved shirt. He wore worn but shined black cowboy boots and had two guns strapped to his waist and legs. He was tall well over six feet, but certainly not as broad as Bo or even Father Callahan. He had sandy-brown hair and twinkling green eyes, he looked good, really good to Lela even if he hadn't shaved in a few days. "What brings you to Trinity, Bo? I thought all you Valley men had already gotten your supplies?" Graham didn't miss a single thing about the two people standing next to Bo. He recognized the brother of Bo dressed in his black Cossack and collar, but not the boy standing next to him. And then the young man looked up, and Graham saw the bluest eyes he had ever seen. This was no boy, this was a woman!

"Graham, it's good to see you and just who we need to talk to." Bo began, "I think you remember my brother, Father Callahan. This young lady standing next to me is Lela Johnson. She came all the way from Paducah, Kentucky to warn the Bellamy's about someone coming to harm them. If you'll remember, the Bellamy's were the family that Rusty was outfitting with a cabin and barn for when they arrived. Well, they came. Getting settled really well, but Ed, the father is not doing so well. Molly says he has a cancer in his stomach."

"Tell me about the people coming to harm them, Miss Johnson." Graham asked her and tipped his hat to her.

"His name if Keifer Kutter...he came to Paducah after the war and invested in a lot of the businesses in town. Before long he owned almost the whole town. He has several saloons...and pleasure houses. He uses drugs, alcohol, and physical force to keep his girls in line." Here Lela hesitated, she really didn't want to tell the entire awful truth about her involvement with Keifer to everybody in town, but she would if it would keep Charlie safe. "He started seeing me...I was flattered that a man of such standing would ever look at someone like me. I thought he had marriage in mind and was courting me. He wasn't. After he had seduced me, he took me back to town. I thought we would get married then, but he had other offers on his mind. He was going to set me up in a house in town and make...other men...pay to sleep with me. I refused, he laughed and said I could work for a while cleaning his saloon.

"The rest of the town considered me a woman of ill-repute since I worked in the saloon. I overheard Keifer telling the bartender that the Bellamy's had moved in the middle of the night. But he was going to find them and bring Charlie back and then Charlie and I would be set up for business. I refused to do the kind of work, he had in mind. I packed up and left in the middle of the night. I've spent the last few weeks riding in rail cars to get here and warn Charlie." She had told the entire tale with her head down and tears rolling down her cheeks. She looked up straight into Graham's eyes. "Will you help keep her safe?"

As soon as Graham had heard the name of Keifer Kutter, it felt like a knife had sliced through his soul and a voice from the past came back. Graham knew Keifer from the War Between the States. He had ridden with William "Bloody Bill" Anderson during the war. They were both members of Quantrill's Raiders. Parts of Kansas would never be the same again because of their ruthless, lawless, and bloody escapades during the war. James and Cole Younger, Frank and Jesse James were also part of his Raiders. They started killing and robbing long before they became such wanted outlaws. He felt drawn to this woman, why he didn't know. But he had got a second chance, he felt she deserved one too. He reached out to gently squeeze her hand. "Yes, ma'am, we'll help keep her safe, and we'll keep you safe, too."

There was much Graham needed to do to get ready to meet up with Keifer Kutter. He knew he wouldn't be coming alone. Trouble was coming to Trinity, and Graham needed to warn the Sheriff, Seth Wheeler and the other Deputy, Ren Kennedy. He also needed to warn his best friends, Jonah McDonald and Andy Renosso. Jonah and Andy knew about Keifer all too well. He watched Bo, Father Callahan, and Lela leave town. Then he went into action. He hadn't been able to stop Keifer ten years ago, but he sure as Hell would now!

CHAPTER 6

Graham went immediately to the Sheriff's office. He was in luck, both Seth and Ren were there. "We got trouble coming to Trinity!" Graham told them and then proceeded to tell them everything he knew about Keifer Kutter. "I grew up in Kansas. I was too young to immediately enlist in the Army in the War Between the States. We had a mix of Southerners and Northerners in Kansas. Some wanted the South to win, and others wanted the North to win. I lived in a little town of Osceola. Most of the people in Osceola were Southerners. My folks weren't but we got along all right with them. One night a bunch of Jayhawkers, Union boys, laid waste to the town. They freed over two hundred slaves, stole three hundred fifty horses, four hundred head of cattle, and three thousand bags of flour, and burned the entire town. All but three of the buildings burned to the ground. My family was in one of those houses. I got out when my pa threw me out the window and then went back to get the rest of the family. I never saw them again. I was young and so angry that anyone could treat civilians that way, I rushed to join the opposite side. Unfortunatcly, that turned out to be the Confederates who were doing the same thing. I was a member of Quantrill's Raiders for all of three days.

"I saw more killing and shooting and ransacking of homes and businesses than I saw in the rest of the war. One of the leaders of the gang was a man called Keifer Kutter. He wasn't as widely known as the Younger brothers or the James brothers, but he was just as vicious. I was with them when they set out to right the wrong done to Osceola, Kansas by going after the town of Lawrence, Kansas. It was a massacre. They killed over one hundred sixty men and boys. There were about four hundred men who rode with Quantrill, and he just turned them loose. It made me sick. I left during the fighting. I wasn't going to be a party to such destruction. I wasn't the only one, there were about a dozen of us who left. We found the Illinois Regulars about a week later and signed up. That's where I spent the rest of the war.

"Keifer disappeared after the war. I thought he was with the James Brothers or even the Younger boys, but it seemed like he wanted to branch out on his own. He settled in Paducah, Kentucky and proceeded to take over the entire town. He seduced a young lady and thought to put her to work in one of his saloons, but she had other ideas. She scrubbed floors and cleaned tables and escaped when she found out he was going after one of her friends to make her into one of his whores in his saloon. She ran off and so did the friend. That friend is the one Rusty Simmons was building the cabin for.

They're both here, and Keifer is bound to come after them. Lincoln may have freed the slaves, but Keifer thinks that the women belong to him since he saw them first. He won't go back empty handed. He'll not come alone either, he'll have about a dozen of his men to back him up. Each and every one of his men are as mean and unconscionable as he is." Here Graham paused, "I told my commanding officer of the Illinois Regulars that I had once been a part of Quantrill's Raiders, he gave me a second chance and the rest of the men with me. I'll understand if you want me to turn in my badge, but I'm not going anywhere. I'll still stay and fight Keifer and all his men. Where do you stand on all of this?" Graham almost held his breath. If they wanted his badge it would just about kill him, he liked being a deputy. He almost felt like his second chance led him here to help as many people as had gotten hurt in Lawrence, Kansas.

The Sheriff looked at his other Deputy and they both nodded their heads, "Hell, Graham, why would I fire one of the best Deputies I've ever had? Of course, you're not fired, and I sure don't want you to turn in your badge with some of the Raiders coming to Trinity! I'd say you turned a pretty awful situation into something to be proud of. I just know that whatever happened in the past, can stay there as far as I'm concerned. I'm only interested in the kind of man you are now. I'm right proud to know you...Now what do we do to stop this madman?"

Graham smiled, he was still a lawman. Now they had to plan. He wouldn't let Keifer do to Trinity as he had to Lawrence and much of Kansas. Nor would he let him get a foothold as a member of the town. In the back of his mind was the image of the bluest eyes he'd ever seen. He had a promise to keep that was for sure.

By this time, Bo, Father Callahan, and Lela had arrived at his cabin. Lela looked around with interest. It was a pretty simple set up, but she could see that it had been built and maintained with loving hands. She smiled to see diapers hanging on line after line of clothes line. She appreciated all the flowers and small trees planted all around the cabin and surrounding ground. She liked the rocker sitting on the porch and the butter churn sitting beside it. Then a tiny little red-headed woman stepped out of the door. She was a beauty and Lela felt dirty and disheveled just looking at her clean dress and apron.

"Father!" The little lady called out to Father Callahan. "It's about time for you to come and see your nephews and namesake! They're almost half-grown! Who's that you have with you?"

"Molly, you're a sight for sore eyes. You just keep getting prettier and prettier. I'd think you'd look old and grey by now being married to my brother!" Father laughed and hugged the little lady. "Molly, I want to introduce Lela Johnson to you. We met on the stage, she's from the same town in Kentucky as the Bellamy's.

She's here to warn them about someone who's coming to harm one of the family."

"Hello, Lela. Welcome to Trinity or at least the Yellowstone Valley of Trinity! Come in and let me get you and Father something to eat and drink and you can tell us why you came and who you're here to warn. It looks like you've traveled a long way and I'm sure that a hot bath would feel good about now." Molly smiled and reached for the hand of Lela, but Lela backed away a few steps.

"Ma'am, I did come a long way to warn my friends, but I can't go into your house without you knowing what kind of woman I am..." Lela hesitated, "I was seduced and worked in a saloon. Only cleaning and washing dishes, but back home no self-respecting citizen would have anything to do with me. I'm not trying to gain any sympathy or anything, I'm just trying to warn you about what I am..." Lela's voice dwindled away. She was looking down at her boots and not at Molly.

"Lela, nothing you've said has changed my mind. Would you like to come in and get something to eat and drink and have a hot bath or not?" Molly smiled at the surprised look that came over Lela's face.

"I'd love to Mrs. Callahan. And thank you for the kind offer." This time she didn't back away when Molly took her hand and led her into her warm and welcoming cabin.

Over the next two hours, Lela and Father Callahan were fed and given an opportunity of taking a hot bath. Father declined but Lela jumped at the chance to feel really clean again, after traveling for five hours in the stagecoach dust she felt like she was wearing half of it. Molly even took one of her dresses out of her backpack and ironed it, so she could stop being a boy and go back to being a young girl again.

Being able to wash all over again was heavenly for Lela, she also took the opportunity to wash her hair again. Getting out of the filthy clothes she had been forced to wear felt so good! Having bound her breasts so no one would suspect her of being a girl, felt great to just be herself again. She dried off and dressed with care back into her own clothes. It felt so good to go back to being Lela Johnson instead of the filthy rag-a-muffin she had been for over three weeks. She sat before the fire drying her beautiful sable hair. It was long and came to almost her waist. Lela listened to the discussion going on at the kitchen table.

There was a knock on the front door. Bo rose to get it. It was none other than Graham Crocker or rather Deputy Graham Crocker! He nodded at all the people sitting at the table and then his eyes rested on Lela. Good Lord, she was beautiful! Graham thought, no wonder Keifer went after her. He smiled at her and then sat down at the table with the others.

"I assume that you're discussing a way to protect those here in the valley and especially the Bellamy's?

That's why I came out. I've talked to both the Sheriff and the other Deputy. Since Keifer wants Charlie and Lela, we think we should have them both stay in town where we can keep an eye on both of them and on the comings and goings of everyone else in Trinity. We would sure appreciate the back-up of all your men and their weapons if and when it'll come to a show-down, but I want to keep as much violence out of your own homes and families as we can. We think this is the best way to go about it. Unless, you have a better idea..."

"What would you do with the two girls in town, Graham?" Molly asked.

"Well, we'd have them both stay in one of the boarding houses in town if we can find one with some extra rooms to let. We'd help them both get jobs, so nothing would seem out of the ordinary to anyone else in town. But we'd have someone watching both of them twenty-four hours of the day. No way will Keifer Kutter and his men be able to come into Trinity without us knowing about it. We will let prominent businesses in town know about them coming, and as soon as they're sighted, we can call up our back-up and meet them before any harm comes to any of us." Here Graham hesitated. "I know who Keifer Kutter is. I met him during the war, he's ruthless and won't hesitate to kill to get his way. The only way to stop him is with a bullet or a badge putting him in jail where he belongs. I've already sent a telegram to the nearest U.S. Marshall's office asking for back-up."

67

Graham waited to see how all of this information was setting with these fine folks. He glanced over at Lela to see how she was feeling about plans being made without asking for her input.

"I'll come with you." Lela announced to the room at large. "The last thing I ever wanted was to bring down trouble on anyone. I appreciate you and the rest of the Sheriff's in your office helping us out with this problem. What kind of work did you have in mind for us to do?" She was steeling herself for him to tell her she was working in another saloon, once a saloon girl always a saloon girl!

"We've got two jobs for the two of you, one will be sewing for the local milliner's dress shop. Her husband is the local handyman around town, but he also served with us in the Army in the war. Andy is a cracker-jack shot and I count on him being able to help keep one of you safe. The other is helping out Jonah McDonald in his General Store. He's had a help-wanted sign up in his store for a long time, so no-one will be the wiser when someone comes and starts helping him at his store. Jonah also served in the war with us, and he's big enough to take on half of Keifer's men single handed! He'll keep the other girl safe. Do either of those jobs appeal to you, Miss Johnson?"

Lela was thrilled! Neither job was in a saloon! "Yes, sir they do. I'm a pretty good seamstress, I think I could work for the milliner's and actually be a help to her in her business...Thank you for finding a job for both of us.

It means a lot to be able to warn Charlie and still be independent as well." Lela had tears in her eyes as she talked to Graham.

"Well, now that that's settled, I'm due over at the Bellamy's to check out Big Ed. Lela do you want to come with me? And of course, Deputy Crocker. Father you might want to come and give Big Ed the Last Rites. I fear he doesn't have long to live..." Molly told him and the room at large.

Bo stepped in, "I think it would be a good idea if we all come. I'll ride around and get all the people in the valley to come too, we can let them all know what's going on and put them on their guard." It took a few minutes to get the twins bundled up and gather enough diapers to keep them dry until they returned. Bo helped Molly into the wagon and handed up the twins, Father Callahan was going to drive. Deputy Crocker helped Lela climb up into the wagon. Crocker's arm still felt warm where she touched it as she climbed the wheel. Graham didn't know what to think about that, but he did like looking at Lela. Surely, there was no harm in that!

Needless to say, the Bellamy's were certainly surprised to see someone from Paducah here in Montana Territory. Lela's arrival caused quite a commotion.

"Lela! I'm so surprised and happy to see you!" Charlie began and hugged Lela in welcome. "I'm at a loss to why you would be here..."

Willa wasn't quite so welcoming. "Did Keifer Kutter send you here, Lela? That is who you work for isn't it?"

She looked with disapproval at Lela and certainly let her feelings about her and her previous job be known. Charlie was confused. Why was her mother being so curt with Lela? They had been friends for years, they went to school together, and their farms were only a few miles apart. What was going on? And why was a man with a star on his vest riding with them?

It was Molly who stepped in to explain, "Willa, we're going to let Lela and Deputy Graham Crocker explain to all of us in a few minutes. But rather than make their explanations several different times, Bo went to ask everyone in the valley to come to your house today, now. This is a problem that we have to solve quickly and with everyone being involved. I think maybe you need to wait before you condemn Lela for what she has or hasn't done." Molly paused, "While we wait for the others, I'm going to go in and look in on Ed...I've brought Bo's brother, Father Callahan, to come with me. He's going to baptize our two boys, Gus, and Lizzy and anyone else who wants it. I thought you might like Father Callahan to give the Last Rites to Ed...We know he's losing ground and has lasted a lot longer than we thought he would. It's your call..."

Willa looked at Molly for several seconds that seemed to stretch on and on. Finally, she nodded her head, "I think seeing Father Callahan will make Ed rest easier. Come on in." She led the way into the cabin for Father and Molly. As Molly walked by Lela, she handed one of her twins to her and the other to Dani who stood behind Charlie.

"Which one of the boys do you have, Lela?" asked Graham. He liked the image of Lela holding a baby.

"I don't know! I can't tell them apart, he's either Joey or Jake!" Lela kissed the soft forehead of the baby she held.

"You have Jake, Lela." Dani told her with a grin, "This is Joey, he has a freckle on the side of his cheek. That's the only way I know to tell which one is which!"

"Charlie, this is Deputy Graham Crocker. He's familiar with our problem and has come to help us come up with a solution. Graham, the tallest woman you see with the golden hair is Charlotte Bellamy, but she goes by the name of Charlie. Danielle Bellamy or Dani as we call her is the other person holding a baby, Josephine Bellamy has platinum white hair, you can't miss her. If I had to make a guess as to where she might be, I would say the barn or anywhere there are animals. Jo has a way with any and all kinds of critters...That was their mother, Willamenia. But we call her Willa. Big Ed is her husband, he's the one who's sick."

"I don't know when I've seen a prettier gathering of young ladies!" Graham told the ladies and tipped his hat to them all. It was about then that wagons started arriving. Lela had never seen so many people come at one time or such a varied group of people loaded into wagons. Without even knowing what she was doing, she stepped closer to Graham, unconsciously knowing that he would keep her safe from any and all of these strangers.

"Howdy, Crocker!" Rusty called out as he pulled up on his horse, followed by Red Dalton on his horse. Tate Adams, Miriam, and Mason pulled up behind him and Miller Smythe, May and Gus could be seen coming over the hill. Bo was riding beside the wagons of the Greer's and the Jackson's. It was everyone in the valley and they were all curious about the emergency that Bo had told them about.

Molly and Willa stepped out of the cabin and smiled at all the friendly faces. Molly reached out and took Joey out of Dani's hands and went and stood by Lela. She was showing her support without saying a word. Lela was so grateful for her faith and nonjudgmental attitude she almost cried. Graham touched her elbow to let her know that he stood beside her not against her. Lela swallowed and tried to smile at all the unfamiliar faces in the crowd. "Good afternoon. I am Lela Johnson. I lived in Paducah with the Ballamy's before they moved. I came to warn Charlie and the rest of the Bellamy's that Keifer Kutter is coming." Lela saw the quick smile on Charlie's face. She is just like I was, thought Lela, I hate to burst her dreams, but I'd rather do that than let her go through what I did.

"Back in Paducah, Keifer Kutter came to see me often. I thought he was courting me, but he wasn't. He only wanted to seduce me and make me into one of his saloon girls...I think another name would be whores. He did seduce me because I thought he was in love with me and wanted to marry me. He took me back to town to his house. He had a maid, a cook, and even a stable boy. It sounded like heaven on earth, but it wasn't. There was no marriage just a stupid farm-girl tricked into giving up her virginity to the wrong man.

"I refused to work in any of Keifer's saloons or pleasure houses. Keifer laughed and told me I could wait tables and clean the floors after everyone was gone. He thought that I would soon change my mind and become one of his...women. I didn't. I had planned my escape very carefully, because Keifer threatened me often enough that I knew if he ever caught me after I ran away, he'd beat me to within an inch of dying. Then he'd drag me back to become one of his whores whether I liked it or not...I saw him use alcohol, drugs, and coercion to keep the other girls jumping to do whatever he wanted." Lela was looking down at the innocent look on Jake's face and didn't want to see the horror or withdrawal of the others.

"I overheard Keifer talking to his bartender one night as I was washing glasses. He was mad that the Bellamy's up and left in the dark of night and no one knew where they went. He said he had spent too much time on flirting with Charlie to let her go, he was going after her just as soon as he found out where she went. He knew that if he put Charlie and me into his home, he could charge whatever amount he wanted for anyone to have a night with either of us."

She heard Charlie's gasp and denial, "I know Keifer, and he wouldn't do that! He loves me!"

"I thought he loved me, too, Charlie. Believe me, if I could have warned you any other way rather than coming out here to tell you, I would have. I don't enjoy parading my sins before a bunch of strangers and friends. But I didn't want you to go through what I did...I tried to talk to my parents, but they have disowned me. They believe what the rest of Paducah does. I'm a fallen woman and one...of...Keifer's women." Here Lela stopped, Graham squeezed her elbow again.

"Most of you know who I am. I'm one of the Deputies in Trinity. What you don't know is that I knew Keifer in the war. He's ruthless, mean, and has absolutely no soft spot for any man, woman, or child. He has several men who work for him that he rode with in the war. I'm sure you heard of his outfit, he was one of the leaders of Quantrill's Raiders." This time there was a collective intake of breath by the entire group. Graham continued, "If Keifer says he'll track down Charlie and now Lela because she had the gumption to leave before she became one of his women, you can bet he'll do just that. He also won't come alone. He'll have at least a dozen of the roughest, meanest sons of bitches you have ever seen. They will take what they want, and to Hell if anyone gets hurt or even killed in the process. I'm here to see that that doesn't happen."

CHAPTER 7

"I will kill that bastard if he even comes close to any of my daughters!" Willa yelled and went to stand near her daughters. It was at that time that Jo decided to show up. Graham couldn't get over the fact that the Bellamy women were all beautiful. Each of them was different, but regardless they were all gorgeous and Keifer would take any one of them for his own.

"Mrs. Bellamy, I believe you, but Keifer won't come knocking on the front door and let you shoot him for the low-life he is. He'll have his men capture Charlie or one of the other of your daughters. They would all be of use to him. We don't want that to happen. Our plan is to split up the girls and take Charlie and Lela to town where we will have someone watch over them twenty-four hours a day. We have jobs lined up for each of them, one as a seamstress and one working in the General Store as a clerk. The husband of the milliner and the owner of the General Store both were in my outfit in the Army in the War Between the States. They've got no quit in them at all, and they both are aware of who and what Keifer is capable of doing." Here Graham paused, he didn't know if the Bellamy's would go along with their plan or not. He didn't want to use force if he didn't want to.

"Seeing your family here with you, we have other problems we have to address. I think that Dani should go and stay with the Smythe's for the time being. They have an infant son and she will be of a lot of help to them. Jo should go and stay with Bo and Molly Callahan. You, Mrs. Bellamy, will stay and take care of your husband, but Red Dalton will be staying here too. He can see to the fields and the garden and the animals, he's also a cracker jack shot. I've worked with Miller and Bo before, and I know they will do everything they can to keep your daughters safe. With your family split-up, it won't be a one stop shop for Kutter to come in and take your whole family with him. He would have no second thoughts of killing both you and your husband to get rid of any witnesses there might be to tell us where they've gone.

"I've talked to the U.S. Marshall's Office and they will be sending us additional men to help apprehend Keifer's entire entourage. I will promise you this, he won't go quietly. They will kill and shoot and burn down as many of you as he can. That's another reason I want Charlie and Lela in town, in town we can see who comes and goes much easier than out here in the country. He and his boys could hide in the woods surrounding your land and you would never know when he was there or when he would make his move. I don't want to see any of you hurt.

77

"Rusty, do you think that you could get word to Boone and his Indian friends to come and watch over you and all the families in the valley? They were a huge help in getting the men that came to get Molly a year or so ago."

"You betcha! Iffn Chief Enapay and his braves get a hold of Keifer or any of his men they'll wish they had never been born! I'll send word to them as soon as I can, Graham. We'll all be on our guard, but to have someone watching our backs so to speak will make us all feel better." Rusty told them and then he turned to Willa, "We'll keep your family safe just like Big Ed wanted us to. It's why he came to the valley isn't it? He knew us all from the war, and every one of us will keep you safe come hell or high water!"

Willa smiled at Rusty and then at Graham. Then she turned to Lela, "I'm sorry about the way I acted when you first came Lela. It took a lot of courage to escape and come and warn us about Keifer. I'm truly sorry for what you've been through. But for the grace of God, it could be the other way around and it could have been my Charlie who was put through what you have been. She could be in the position of trying to escape and warn you. You will always have a place in my prayers for what you have done for us all." Then she went over and hugged Lela, baby and all!

Tears came pouring down Lela's face, "Thank you! Thank you, Mrs. Bellamy, so much. You don't know how much that means to me to have you...forgive me and treat me like you've always done in the past."

At that moment, Father Callahan poked his head out the doorway of the cabin, "Molly, Willa, I think you should come right away! Something is not quite right with Ed!" They all moved as one toward the door.

Something had indeed happened to Ed; one side of his face was drawn down toward his chin. He wasn't able to talk or to focus his eyes. Molly had handed Joey to Bo and stood beside his bed checking out what other functions had been diminished. She listened to his heart and his labored breathing. She shook her head, "It seems that Ed has had a stroke and a heart attack. He has no control over the left side of his body. I doubt that he'll be able to talk to you any more...I'm afraid that the end is very near. Willa, if you and your girls would like to say good bye to Ed in private, Father Callahan and I will go into the other room...I don't think I would take too much time...his time here on earth is very short." Molly patted Big Ed's hand and Willa's shoulder as she passed and then she and Father Callahan went into the other room to tell the others what had happened and what to expect. They were all sorry to see one of their own die, but they also knew how much he had been suffering these last few weeks.

Tate took charge, they would dig a hole near where April's body was buried. Sam and Calvin would build a box to put his remains. Each man kissed his wife as they were leaving. Bo gave Joey back to Molly and they were gone. The women talked among themselves as to how best to help Willa and the girls. It seemed like only minutes when Willa and her daughters came out of the room. They were all quietly crying and holding onto each other. When Willa's eyes met Molly's, she shook her head. That's when they all knew that Big Ed had passed away.

Molly took charge, "Willa, I'm going to send you and Father Callahan to go back in and wash and prepare Ed for burial. I know it's very soon, but it's warm, and bodies don't keep very long in this weather. We will bury Ed today and Father Callahan will bless his soul and give him a nice funeral." She saw both Willa and Father Callahan nod their heads and go back into the bedroom. "The rest of us will have to take care of the other arrangements. Jo and Mason, will you both go out and gather as many wildflowers as you can. I think the flowers will make your father happy and the rest of your family. Charlie, pack your belongings. As soon as we bury your father, you will be going back to town with Lela and Graham. Dani, would you pick out a nice quilt or blanket that we can wrap your father in?" At her nod, Molly continued, "The rest of us will go to our homes and get whatever food we can gather and bring it back here for a meal after the funeral. "Friends stick close-by whenever there's been a loss in the community, we will too."

Graham drove the wagon back to the Callahan's home. He held one of the boys while Lela held the other

80

when Molly went into the cabin to get what they needed. He had never held a baby in his life, and he was holding it like it was going to break! Lela found the first humorous thing to laugh about today and in quite a long time. Her laughter washed over Graham like soft tinkling bells. It was refreshing and beautiful. He hoped to make Lela laugh more often in the coming weeks. Molly came back carrying a large pan of chili and several loaves of bread. She laughed at the way Graham was holding Joey and took him out of his relieved hands.

"I thank you, Mrs. Callahan, I was sure worrying about what I would do if he started squirming around. I was afraid I would drop him!" Graham confessed to the two women he sat between on the wagon seat.

"Have you never been around children before, Deputy?" Molly asked smiling.

"Nope! Never! I was the youngest in my family...they all died in a fire leaving only me to survive. Most of my friends aren't married and those that are don't have a lot of children. It just never came up. It's not that I don't like children, I've just never had the chance to be around them, especially little babies." He told them all the while watching how easily both of the women held the infants in their arms.

Within a few hours, Sam and Calvin had the burial box made for Big Ed. He had been washed and dressed in his one and only suit and carefully laid to rest in the quilt lined box. The men carried the coffin to the hole they had prepared on the hill overlooking the valley. Willa and her daughters noted that there was already a headstone on another grave on the hill. It read 'April Smythe, born 1856, died 1871.' Flowers that Jo and Mason had picked covered both April's grave and all around where Ed would be laid to rest. It was simple but beautiful in its simplicity.

Father Callahan read from the Bible and blessed Ed's remains. Then he picked up a hand of dirt and said, "From dust we all came and to dust we will return." He sprinkled the dirt over Ed's grave and he gave the nod for each of Ed's family to do the same. Rusty also picked up a handful of the dirt and dropped it on his friend's gravesite. Father Callahan started singing 'Amazing Grace' in a lovely baritone, the rest of the valley joined in. It was over in a very short time. They all walked back to the cabin in silence. They ate quickly and cleaned up the dishes.

Graham was the first to leave with the two women and Rusty in his wagon. Red had gone back to their cabin and brought over some clothes to stay with Willa in her cabin. Jo handed up a pillowcase of clothes to Bo to put in their wagon and then sat in the back while Father Callahan, Molly, Bo and the twins loaded up and headed out. The Greer's and Jackson's followed them down the hill. Dani came out of the cabin, hugged her mother and climbed into Miller's waiting wagon. Tate nodded his head at Willa and Red and told them they would be watching and would come as soon as they were needed, and then he and his family headed for home. They each had children to be put to sleep, animals to be seen to, clean clothes to be taken off the lines, and a cabin to be made safe from any and all intruders.

Red saw to the animals in the barn of Willa's. He stacked wood on the porch and in every wood box. Then he headed back to Rusty and his cabin. He milked the cow, gathered the eggs, cleaned out the stalls, and loaded up enough wood for Rusty to keep warm for the night. A lot of responsibility had fallen on his young shoulders keeping the Bellamy's home and mother safe. But he still had Rusty who had been like a father to him to watch out for. He felt he was man enough to take care of them both.

CHAPTER 8

Graham was trying to prepare the two young ladies for what to expect when they got to town. "We're going to change your names when we get to town. There aren't that many Lela's or women going by the name of Charlie out here. Lela you will become Leah Jones, and Charlie you will become Lottie Bell. It's the best we could come up with on such short notice." Graham explained and made sure that Rusty was aware of where they were going and where they would be staying. "Both of you are slim and shapely ladies, that too will have to change. A few well-placed pillows to hide your shape will help tremendously. You will both wear spectacles to help hide your faces. We're going to trust that to hide you in plain sight will be the best way to keep you safe." He waited for both of the girls to nod, Lela smiled and nodded quickly, not so with Charlie.

"What if I don't want to be fat and ugly when we go to town? I wouldn't want everyone's first impression of me to be so terrible! Why, there has to be a lot of eligible bachelors in town. How will I ever find a beau looking like that?! No, I'm afraid it just won't do. You'll have to think of something else." Charlie told the astonished Deputy and Rusty. Then she proceeded to straighten out her dress, so it wouldn't get wrinkled and then started to primp her hair.

Graham started to tell her just how it was going to be, but Rusty beat her to it. "Listen up little princess, your pa is dead! Life for you is going to change! A lot of decent people are putting their lives on the line to keep you safe! This isn't a time for trying to catch young men's eyes on how pretty you are! We want to do just the opposite! We want them and every other low life that comes through Trinity to gloss right over you and Lela! We don't want them remembering a beautiful blonde that works in the store and report back to his boss about you. Your pa came to Trinity to keep you safe, and that's exactly what we're going to do. Iffn I have to turn you over my knee to make you behave and do what they want you to do, you can bet your bottom dollar, that's exactly what I'll do!"

Never in all her life had anyone spoken to Charlie like Rusty just did! "Well...well...we'll just see about that! My family won't stand for my being treated to such abuse from you!" Charlie told him in a near shout.

"Guess again!" Rusty told her, "The last words your pa spoke to me was for me to find a way to keep his girls safe no matter what it takes, and by God we're going to do it! Iffn Graham tells you to pad your body with pillows, you'll do it! Iffn he tells you to wear spectacles and change your name, you'll do it! You are not the one calling the shots around here. They arc! And until those animals are caught, you'll continue to do exactly that.

Do you understand, or do I stop this here wagon and tan your behind to make you into a believer?"

Graham could hardly hide the smile that came to his face at the way Charlie was reacting to Rusty's blunt words. Jonah would have his hands full with this one, that was for sure! He was glad he had Lela to watch over carefully. She seemed much more manageable. Finally, Charlie nodded her head, but her eyes were still defiant at the very idea that anyone would find her anything but desirable was just too much to fathom!

Ren Kennedy was waiting for them just outside of town. He tipped his hat to the two ladies and spoke to Rusty and Graham. "We've had a change of plans, Graham. There're no rooms to rent in any of the rooming houses or boarding houses in town. I know, I've been to every single one trying to find safe accommodations for the two girls. But the Sheriff has come up with another plan that I think will work. Jonah has a room in his store that he was going to board his new help in. The young lady who works for him will stay in his upstairs rooms and he will sleep in the room below. He'll hear anything or anyone that even tries to come into his store, and nothing will ever get by Jonah to get to her." He waited for Graham's approval before he went on. Graham nodded.

"The other girl will have to stay in your house, Graham. You can pretend to be married, but that's the only other spare room we have in this whole town. There's two bedrooms in your house and you can each have one of them. You'll walk her to work each day and hand her over to Andy, and at the end of the day he'll either walk her home or you'll come and get her. Iffn you're worried about her good name, get married for the time being. After all this is over with, you can have the marriage annulled quickly enough and no one will be the wiser. What do you think?" He kept sending glances at the two beautiful women in the back of the wagon. Whoopee! Those were sure two good looking women sitting back there. He wouldn't mind being married for good with either one of them!

Graham didn't say anything for a few minutes. He was mulling over in his mind if there were any other options available to any of them. Being that close to Lela all the time could sure prove unsettling to his peace of mind, but if that were the only way, he'd do it. "Lela, you've heard everything that Ren told us, are you willing to marry me in name only to keep you safe?"

Lela didn't hesitate, "Yes, I will do just about anything to keep Charlie and myself out of the hands of Keifer. Thank you for not objecting to an impossible situation. I thank the rest of you too. I will do whatever you ask, no questions asked. Just tell me what to do." Charlie looked at her friend as if she had never seen her before! How could she be so meek and willing to fall in with their hairbrained ideas? Being made to work in Keifer's saloon must have been harder on her than she thought.

"Thank you, Lela, pretending to be married to you won't be too hard to do, trust me!" Graham told her and found her to be blushing. "But I will warn you. I just bought the house in town. It's rough and not too clean, but I will make it safe for you, I promise."

Lela smiled and nodded her head. In the back of her mind was the thought that it couldn't be any worse than living in a backroom of the saloon and having to bar the door each night to keep out any unwanted visitors. At least with Graham there she would feel safe.

"All right, that means we have to alter our plans." Graham began taking charge, "Rusty, pull up into the alley behind Jonah's store. We'll smuggle the girls in through the back door and get disguised. Then I'll take 'Leah' over to the nearest preacher to marry us. And then take her home with me. I'll leave 'Lottie' for Jonah to take care of. He can lay out any rules he wants her to follow to keep her safe and still help him out in the store." He waited for everyone to give them their acceptance of his proposal. He looked long and hard at Charlie before she nodded. *God help you Jonah!* Graham thought as he rode to the Mercantile.

After Graham had left him this morning telling him about the coming of Keifer Kutter to their quiet little haven, Jonah couldn't think straight. He had only been a young man when the Quantrill's Raiders had come to Lawrence, Kansas. He had watched them kill his uncle and try to carry out everything of any value from the store. He had grabbed a gun and tried to kill every last one of them before they sent a bullet his way. Thankfully, it only grazed his head. When he woke up, he was surrounded by about a dozen boys all about his age. They were cleaning up his head as best they could.

"Boy, you must have shit for brains to think that your one gun would do anything but get yourself killed against those Raiders!" The tallest one of the boys spoke.

"I guess I wasn't thinking, "Jonah mumbled. "I just reacted, that's all." He looked around to where he was. He wasn't in Lawrence that was for sure. "Where exactly am I? I gotta get back and bury my uncle!" He tried to get up but the pain in his head made him fall back with a groan.

"You are not going anywhere for a few days. Your head took quite a jolt when the bullet grazed it. You also lost a lot of blood. We're hidden about three miles from Lawrence. The Raider's have left, but then they didn't leave much behind. They killed every man and boy in town and burned just about every building they could find. We're not going back, but forward. We'll join the first legitimate Army we come across and join the fight against the Raider's and the rest of the Confederate Army. It's their fault to let such ruthless and random killing happen to civilians. The North isn't much better, they do have the Jayhawkers, but I have never seen such enjoyment in killing as I did as I watched those Raider's. I...we...won't be a party to it." Spoke up one boy. He wasn't as tall as the one bandaging his head, but you could tell he was their leader just by the way he carried himself. "My name is Graham Crocker. What's yours?" Graham had held out his hand for Jonah to shake, it began a friendship that held to this day.

"Jonah...Jonah McDonald." Jonah managed to say, "Thanks for saving my life back there. If you don't mind, I'll go along with you to fight the Rebels. Maybe someday I'll meet up with the men who killed my uncle. Maybe I'll be man enough to get justice for my uncle then."

The others teased him about being only half-grown and that he was only half a man. But as they joined up with the Illinois Regulars and trained to fight, they found that the half-grown boy was full of grit and determination. He did grow to be a man, a very large man, in the Army. He also kept the friendship with Graham and many of the others after the war. They moved with him to Trinity and helped drive and load the many teamster wagons he brought with him to set up his store. His uncle had left everything to Jonah, but Lawrence held too many memories that Jonah didn't want to remember. He was a different man, he would go to a place that they never had to remember the Jayhawkers or Quantrill's Raiders for the rest of his life. He knew that he no longer resembled the boy back in Lawrence, but he could still vividly see the face of the man who had killed his uncle. He even knew his name...Keifer Kutter had killed his uncle, raided the store, and laughed at the young boy who tried to shoot him. Yes, Jonah thought, he would finally git his revenge on the man who had ruined his whole world.

His first thought as Graham entered through the back door was that he had two very pretty girls with him. He shut the front door and put up the sign that he would be back in an hour. Then he headed for the room he had made for his new clerk in the back of the store. Lela and Charlie both looked up as the door was opened. Jonah's entire frame filled the entire doorway. Charlie gasped at the size of Jonah and edged back a little more into the room. Graham reached out his hand and shook Jonah's, so did Rusty.

"Jonah, the brunette is Lela Johnson, but we're going to call her Leah. We're going to get married tonight and she'll be staying in my house. So, you might want to call her Leah Crocker whenever you see her. The blonde is Charlotte Bellamy, also called Charlie, and as of today she will now be called Lottie Bell, your new clerk and houseguest. What do you have in mind for disguises?" Graham asked him.

"Well, I went to the resale shop down the street and bought some dresses for...lack of a better word, larger sized ladies. I've put several pillows of various sizes on the bed to try out. You told me to get some glasses for the two women, one of them to be tinted. They're on the table by the pitcher of water. I even bought two hats they can wear to cover their hair when they do go out. I don't know much about women's wear except what I sell in my store, so I'm not promising anything about how they will look in the clothes."

"Thank you, Mr. McDonald, for going to all the trouble for us. I...we...appreciate it very much. Don't we Charlie or rather Lottie?" Leah told him softly. Jonah noticed her brilliant blue eyes and immediately told her to wear the tinted glasses.

"You have the got the brightest blue eyes I've ever seen, they're memorable. You are going to have to keep them covered with the tinted glasses, ma'am. They're something no red-blooded male would ever forget." Jonah told her with a grin.

That's when Charlie spoke up, "Those are the ugliest dresses I've ever seen! I won't wear anything that will make me look so bad! It's bad enough that I have to wear pillows to hide my shape, but I'll do so with style!"

"Can you sew?" Jonah asked her staring at her intently.

"Well, of course I can sew, why do you ask?" Charlie wanted to know. He was certainly asking such personal questions.

"Then make your own clothes in the manner and style you want, but until then you will wear those dresses or stay locked up in the four rooms upstairs." Jonah told her in a no-nonsense voice. "This is my store, my inventory, you will do what I say and not what you want. Is that understood?"

Charlie stuck out her chin in a stubborn stance and stood up to Jonah nose to nose, "And what if I don't do what you say?"

"Then I'll do what every other man in the position of power in his household would do...I'll lock you in your room until you come to reason. I'm not negotiating, 'Lottie Bell', you'll do whatever it takes to keep you safe. Do we understand each other?"

The idea of being locked in a room all day long every day did not appeal to Charlie, so she sullenly nodded her head. She hated having to deal with such bossy men! Maybe when Jonah saw how capable she was in his store, he would relent his rigid medieval ideas on what she could and could not do. Jonah McDonald didn't know who he was dealing with, Charlie thought to herself. The men left the room leaving the two girls to get dressed into the larger sized dresses.

They took off their current dresses and held up the large dresses. A chuckle erupted from first Lela and then Charlie. They helped each other get dressed in the best of the stack of clothes on the bed. They positioned a pillow in the front of each of them and one giving them a much larger derriere. They then slipped the gowns over them and tied them with the sashes that had been provided. Then Lela arranged Charlie's hair in a rather severe bun at the back of her head, and Charlie did the same to hers. They slipped on the glasses and were amazed at the image they both now portrayed. Lela put on a bonnet and folded two more of the dresses and her own over her arm. She was ready to leave. Charlie wasn't happy with the way she looked. She wasn't used to not turning heads everywhere she went. They opened up the door to let the men see the finished results.

Graham smiled as he looked at Lela and grabbed her hand. "Are you ready to go get hitched, Leah? And then I'll introduce you to the Renosso's. Annalise is married to Andy Renosso and owns the milliner's shop. Then I'll take you to your new home."

Rusty took one look at Charlie and burst out laughing, "Well, Princess, it looks like you have your work cut out for yourself making yourself some new clothes. I definitely don't think anyone would recognize you looking like that!"

"Oh...o...o...o! You buffoon!" Lottie yelled at him. Jonah put a hand on her shoulder and turned her around until she was looking at him.

"You'll do, Lottie. Let me take you upstairs to your new living quarters. You can make yourself at home and get yourself situated tonight. Tomorrow will be soon enough to be introduced as my new clerk. Gather up all your clothes from back home and those I picked out for you. Good night Rusty, you take care getting home before it gets dark. Say Hello to all the folks back in the valley. Let them know that we've got things under control here in Trinity." Jonah told Rusty and let him out the back door, so he could leave. He was still chuckling as he walked out. But he did manage to tell

Jonah 'Good Luck with that one' as he walked out the door.

Jonah privately agreed! Charlie Bellamy was not going to go quietly into her disguise. But Jonah had dealt with difficult people every day, one more couldn't be all that much trouble. He headed upstairs to get Lottie settled.

Charlie took one look at the four rooms upstairs and wanted to cry! There was no way she could ever live here in these dirty, filthy rooms! There were two bedrooms, one had a bed, but it had a sheet over the mattress and one thin blanket covering it. It looked like it hadn't been made...ever! This room did have a dresser or rather armoire and that was it...no rug, no curtains, no wash stand! Charlie thought she was living in hell! The parlor was non-existent. It consisted of the ugliest couch she had ever seen and a single chair. Both were situated in front of the fireplace or rather pot-bellied stove.

But the kitchen was the worst. It had a table, two chairs, and a stove. Charlie saw no dishes, no supplies to cook with, nothing at all to make this even appear to be welcoming. The other bedroom was empty and dusty just like everything else. She heard footsteps coming up the stairs. Just wait until she had a few minutes telling Jonah McDonald what she thought about his home!

Jonah McDonald had barely opened up the door to his parlor when Charlie started in about how horrible his home was and she wouldn't and couldn't live in such squalor! "You will just have to find a better place for me to live." Charlie told him in a near shout. "It's filthy up here. When was the last time it was cleaned?"

Jonah wasn't in the mood to be yelled at. He turned on his heel and went back downstairs and grabbed a bucket, some lye soap, a broom, and some rags. He was back up with a broom, the bucket, soap, and rags. These he handed to Charlie. "If you don't like living in such filth, then clean it to where it will meet with your high standards, Princess. It'll give you something to do tonight while I finish up in the store."

"This is your house!" Charlie yelled, "Why should I have to clean your filth?"

"You find it dirty. You clean it. I don't spend much time up here, I'm always so busy in the store. So, since this will be your home for the foreseeable future, I suggest you make it to fit your requirements. Good Luck!" Jonah turned to leave and go back downstairs to finish his work in the store, "I'll get something for us to eat from the eatery across the street and bring it up when I close for the night." And then he was gone.

Charlie stewed and walked up and down the rooms. She had wanted so badly to get away from the ranch in the valley, and when she did manage to leave, she came to an even worse situation! What was she going to do? She sat down at the kitchen table and put her head in her hands. She was too mad to cry, and she knew that she had too much pent-up anger to just sleep or sit in a chair for the rest of the night. She gave a huge sigh and took off the over-sized dress and pillows and changed into some pants and a shirt. She even took off her shoes and went barefoot. She refused to live in such filth, and she decided that the only way it was going to change was if she made the changes. So be it, she would show that know-it-all McDonald that she was just as stubborn as he was. He said she could make it livable, she would do just that. She was after all living above a Mercantile that sold everything, she would need to make this place into a home. She rolled up her sleeves and went to work.

"I now pronounce you man and wife." The grey-haired minister told Graham and Leah. "You may kiss the bride, Mr. Crocker!" The minister turned to finish filling out the paperwork on the marriage certificate.

Graham grinned at Lela, "Well, you heard what the minister said..." He leaned down and gently kissed Lela's lips. She didn't pull away and looked up at him with the most confused look in her eyes. Graham couldn't stop himself from kissing her again. Then he pulled away, paid the minister, and grabbed Lela's hand. "Let's go meet your employer, shall we?"

"I'd like that," Lela said in a very soft voice.

Together they walked to the Renosso's store and home. The shop was at the front of the home and their home was towards the back of the store. Luck was with them, both Annalise and Andy were home when they arrived.

"Knock, Knock!" Graham said as they both entered the door. Both Annalise and her husband Andy came from the back of the store to greet them. Annalise was tiny and very pregnant! Andy wasn't much taller but heavily muscled. They were both smiling.

"Oh, I'm so glad you've come to help me in the store! I feared that I would be sewing all through labor with no one to see to the store or get my orders finished in time. Andy told me not to worry, that everything would work out and sure enough, here you are!" Annalise never stopped smiling as she showed Leah where she would be working, the patterns, the material, the mannikins to help with the shape of the garments, and the sewing machine. Leah reached out and carefully touched the machine.

"I always wanted a sewing machine, but they were much too expensive, and I couldn't afford one. Imagine working in a place where I can watch you sew on one!" Leah told her.

"Oh, no, I can't get close enough to work the foot pedals with this protruding stomach. You'll be the one using the machine." Annalise told her.

"I can't wait to start!" Leah's joy showed in her face. Graham couldn't look away. Even dressed in clothes too large and with her hair pulled back severely and even from behind tinted lenses, she was beautiful. Not just on the outside, but inside where it counted. He would have to watch his heart with this one, Graham thought.

The girls started talking about sewing and even about when Annalise was due with her baby. Leah felt like she had known her for a long time, not that she had just met her a few minutes ago. She was going to like working with her sewing. Andy and Graham talked in low voices on the other side of the room.

"Annalise looks like she likes Leah." Graham told him.

"What's not to like? She's pretty and seems really nice. I don't mind telling you I'll breathe easier knowing that Annalise won't be alone anymore. I always worried that I would be working on a job half way across town when her labor started, and she would be all alone to give birth to our child. Having Leah here, will at least give me peace of mind that she can run get the doctor or me at least at the first sign of labor." Andy told him with a smile, "How's the other girl?"

"Let's just say that Jonah is going to have his hands full with that one, she's beautiful, but she's spoiled and won't be so easy to live with, that's for sure!" Graham told him about the remarks made by Charlie in the wagon and even once they arrived at the Mercantile. Andy shook his head, glad she wasn't his problem!

CHARTER 9

Graham and Leah walked to where he lived. He was a little embarrassed that it wasn't nicer or bigger than it was. But he was a bachelor, his needs were few. When the tiny house went on the market, Graham had jumped at the chance to move out of the boarding house he had been living for the last six years. He was tired of living with other people he didn't know. The house fit his needs to a tee. But he worried about it not being what Leah would like.

Leah's first impression of Graham's home was that it was cozy. Granted it needed a good cleaning, but the four rooms were decent sized and wouldn't take that much work to make it really nice. She broke the silence and turned to Graham, "It's nice, Graham. I can't wait to get to work cleaning and making it our temporary home. Thank you for doing all of this for me, and for Charlie too."

"No thanks are necessary, Leah. I've been wanting to put Keifer Kutter away for a long, long time. Using you and Charlie as bait will make that possible. Now what do you need in the way of supplies to make this place livable?"

"Well, most married couples cook in their homes. You have a really good cook stove, so I guess I'll need food supplies. I can cook, so you won't starve! Are there dishes and pots and pans here in the house?" Leah asked him.

"I think it's what you see is what you have! I guess we'll need to go back to the Mercantile tonight and get us some supplies. Look through the rest of the house and get a feel for what we will need to make this into a home. I've got money saved, so don't scrimp. Believe me, I'm going to enjoy coming home to a clean house and good meals waiting for me, not to mention a pretty little woman standing over the stove doing all the work!" Graham was trying to make her smile and relax.

Leah did just that. She walked through the home and noted what it did have and what it did not have. She took out paper and pencil from her own backpack and started writing down what she needed. She even walked out the back door to see what they had in the back yard. She sighed at the long list of needs and went back to report to Graham.

"It's a good thing you have some money, Graham, we will need a lot to get started. I won't try to buy out the store, but in order to make you three meals a day and be able to clean the house and wash our clothes, it's going to take a tidy sum...Would you mind if we took the old mattresses out and put in some new ones?" She hesitated, "We can make new ones out of a couple of old sheets sewn together on three sides and fill them with fresh cut grasses. It will smell great and be a lot softer than what's on them now."

"I don't mind, I wasn't too fond of the mattress either, but I didn't know how to change it. There's a resale store that Jonah bought all the large dresses from, we'll check there first to see what we might be able to find. That should save us some money." Graham turned to Leah, "Do you mind getting used instead of new?"

"Are you kidding? I will be thrilled to get whatever we can find for a lower price! Remember that I lived on a farm and in the back room of a saloon before I came here. On the farm, we made do with what we had. And in the saloon, even trying to clean that room after working fourteen hours a day, was just more than I could manage. This will be heavenly!" Leah smiled at Graham. Graham smiled back. He was going to enjoy living here with her, maybe too much. Together they left to borrow a wagon from Jonah to load up all their purchases from the resale store and his.

Leah's first impression of the resale store was that it was dirty, very dirty. Her second impression was that it was a gold mine for what they needed. Leah found sheets they could use on mattresses and for the beds, too. She found several blankets and even several quilts. Some needed some repair work, but she was an excellent seamstress and that could be taken care of quickly. Graham found some pots and pans that included a large pot they could use to heat up water for bathing. Leah found a wash board and two rollers that would help wring out the clean clothes. Leah also found some pretty dishes that would work very well for them as well as some knives and silverware.

Graham found two rockers and a table and four chairs. Leah was thrilled with his finds. She was holding on to several wooden spoons and a soup ladle and some bowls to use in her baking. She also found several different sized pots with lids that she could use to put her flour and sugar in on the counter. Of course, she didn't have a counter yet or a cabinet to hold all their supplies, but she hoped that Andy would be able to come over and help build them for her in the very near future.

From the resale shop, they went to the Mercantile. Jonah was surprised to see them so soon, but Graham explained that they were making the house into a home just like other newlyweds would be doing. Jonah nodded and started writing down all the supplies that Leah needed to begin cooking their meals. While Jonah started gathering all the foodstuffs, Leah went to look over material that she could make some curtains out of and an oilcloth to cover their new table. Graham picked up an axe to start chopping wood with, a scythe to cut the grass around the house, and a shovel. He also asked Jonah to add on a bag of lime to put down the outhouse. It needed a good cleaning and anything else to make it smell better. Then he picked up a hammer and a box of nails. No telling what all he'd need to be doing to make it a better place for both of them to live.

Graham helped Jonah load up all the purchases into the wagon and then helped Leah get into the wagon. He settled up with his friend and they left. They had a lot to accomplish before they went to bed tonight. Leah had them stop at Annalise's store to use the sewing machine to sew up the seams on the mattresses. She told Graham that she would close the seams once they had been filled with grass. She also broached the subject of having Andy come over and make her a kitchen counter and shelves to store all the supplies. Graham thought that it was an excellent idea and while Leah sewed up the seams, he talked Andy into coming over tomorrow when he brought Leah home and build whatever she wanted.

While Graham filled the mattresses, she started cleaning the house and making them some dinner. Graham agreed, he didn't like leaving her for that long, but he felt they had time before Keifer or his men showed up. He couldn't get over the joy that Leah gave him. Just finding all their loot as she called it in the resale shop was fun. They both laughed as they carried in all their purchases.

Leah immediately changed into a pair of pants and an old shirt, the same she had traveled in for two weeks coming here. Molly had washed them out while she was taking a bath at her home. It hadn't taken them long to dry in the gentle wind that blew earlier today. Leah filled the bucket with water and shaved some lye soap into it and began by scrubbing every single one of the floors in the house. Then she used a broom to knock down any cobwebs in the corners. She rolled up the two mattresses that were already on the two beds and dragged them out the back door. She poured the bag of lime down the outhouse and then went back into the house to get her scrub bucket to wash down the outhouse, too!

By the time Graham came back with the two mattresses filled with grass, the house already smelled better than it had. Leah had put the tablecloth on the table and had started supper. She fried up potatoes and had made some biscuits. That with making them ham steaks made up the meal. Graham was thrilled. It was a lot better than any of the food in the eateries around them. While they were eating, they talked.

"Graham, would you mind stretching that rope we bought at the resale shop to give me several clothes lines tonight after supper? That way I can start washing tomorrow morning and make up some bread before we both leave for work. I'll take it down when I come home for the day."

"That should be no problem. While you're doing the dishes, I'll use my new scythe to cut the grass around the house and outhouse. There's a small shed out back that I'll use to house my tools. I'll pick up a small saw tomorrow and cut a hole in the front and back door of the outhouse and cover it with fine mesh. It shouldn't take too long for it to smell a lot better!"

"That would be great, Graham! I already put the lime down it and scrubbed it clean when I did the floors." Leah hesitated, "I like the rockers in front of the fireplace in the parlor. It makes the whole house look homier."

"I always liked the idea of sitting in a rocker on a cold wintry evening and smoking my pipe while the little woman sewed beside me. It's what my ma and pa always did while I was growing up..."

"Well, I'll definitely be sewing in that rocker for many a night! I'll take the curtain material with me tomorrow and sew them up before I come home. I don't like the idea of people looking in the windows at us. I would like to have more privacy. Do you mind?"

"Hell, no! I don't particularly like people watching me either." He chuckled, "Putting your 'large' dresses over the windows tonight was a smart move on your part!"

Leah laughed with him. "I didn't know what else to do! I didn't want people watching me in my old clothes as I scrubbed the floors, and the dresses were just lying there, so...I improvised!"

Having the dresses act like curtains certainly made the rooms more private, but they did look kind of silly laying over the thin rods holding them up over the windows. Leah did the dishes while Graham filled the wood boxes and hung clothes lines for her outside. Then he started cutting down all the tall weeds that surrounded the little house. It was almost dark when

Graham went back inside. Leah was sewing the mattresses closed in one of the rockers. She gave two pillowcases to Graham. "Would there be enough grass to fill these two pillowcases? We can use them as pillows if it's alright with you?" Graham smiled and took the two cases.

"It's a great idea, I'm surprised that we didn't think of it before!" Laughing he went outside to fill them up.

Leah finished one of the mattresses and stopped to put it on Graham's bed. Then she put on sheets and a blanket and a quilt. It looked warm and inviting. She looked around at the clothes on the floor. Maybe she could talk Graham to putting a few nails in the walls to hang the clothes. One step at a time, Leah thought as she went back to closing her mattress. That bed was certainly going to feel good tonight!

Leah was a fast seamstress and a good one. She had her mattress sewn shut just as Graham came in the door with the two pillowcases. She continued to sew them shut while he put some nails in the wall to hang his clothes and hers. By the time she was done and had the pillowcases closed as well, Graham was done as well. All their clothes were hanging up on the walls and both beds were made. Graham watched while Leah made a trip to the outhouse, and then followed her into the house. Together they closed up the house for the night and made sure the cook stove was ready for the morning, and the pot-bellied stove was loaded for the night. It was late spring in Montana, but the nights were still cold.

Morning found them both up and ready for the day. Before Graham even knew it, Leah had made up several loaves of bread and was washing out all their dirty clothes on the back porch. The large pots they had bought worked out very well. When she was done, she started on their breakfast and making them both sandwiches for their lunches. She also planned what she would cook for dinner that night.

"Graham, do we have an account at the Mercantile that I can use to buy meat for dinner tonight or any other night?"

"We don't, Leah, but I'll go talk to Jonah first thing this morning and set one up. If there's something that we need go ahead and get it. I'll settle up with him once a week from now on. I'll be saving all kinds of money not having to buy breakfasts, lunches or dinners at all the eating places up and down the boardwalk. It'll also be nice to not have to pay anyone to wash out my clothes every couple of weeks thanks to my hard-working wife!" Graham told her and winked at her.

Leah blushed and smiled, it may only be temporary, but it was fun being married to Graham. He was quite a man.

All too soon they were packed up and ready to go to work. Leah had all the curtain material and measurements to make them at work. She also had several of the dresses from the windows to adjust to fit her better. She was looking forward to working with Annalise today and using the sewing machine. She also couldn't wait to tell Andy what she wanted him to build for her in their house. She hoped that by the time Graham came home tonight, she would have curtains up, real curtains! And she hoped to have all the dishes, pots, pans, bowls, and all the supplies put away on shelves. She also was going to see if he could put in a half-barrel tub like the one at Molly Callahan's. One that didn't require them to bail out the water bucket by bucket!

Graham dropped her off at the Renosso's, nodded at Andy that she was now under his guardianship, and then surprised Leah with a kiss as he walked out the door. You could hear him whistling as he walked away. Leah blushed and then asked Annalise what she wanted her to do first.

"Before we even get started, why don't you sew up your curtains and tell Andy what you want done at your home today. That way, he can get started and so can we. I can't imagine not having anything up to cover the windows!" Annalise told her with a cringe.

"Well, neither did I, so I covered the windows with my dresses so we could have some privacy! They looked pretty silly hanging over the windows, but it worked! Unfortunately, I needed one of them to wear today. I appreciate being able to use your machine to get them done. It shouldn't take me long to finish them." Leah began. "Andy, I would like several things built. One is a kitchen counter with shelves under them to hold all my pots and pans and dishes. I'd also like a shelf above the counter to put glasses and such in. Then I'd like a book shelf like structure to hold all our supplies. It needs to be deep enough to hold three of the wooden crates we brought all the supplies home in. I thought I could slide three of them in side by side on the three bottom shelves for potatoes, onions, carrots, sweet potatoes, flour, corn meal, sugar, rice, and beans. The shelves above the staples can be narrower, but I still want to be able to put in quart jars of vegetables and fruit."

"None of that should be a problem, Leah." Andy told her admiring her for knowing what she wanted. "Is there anything else?"

"Yes, but I don't know if it's possible." She paused, "When I was at the Callahan's they used a really large half-barrel as a bath tub. They had a hose hooked to the bottom and just pulled the cork to let the water drain out. It was heavenly to not have to drain it bucket by bucket! I was also wondering if you could also put a small sink in the kitchen counter that I could also pour out water from scrubbing or cooking without throwing it outside to make things muddy. Are they both doable?"

"No problem, it might take me longer than one day to get it all done, but I know they are both doable! When I drain the tub and the sink, are you going to have a garden in back to send all that water to?" Andy asked kissing his own wife as he was loading up his tools.

"Well, after I leave work today, I'm going to go to the Mercantile and get some seeds and meat for the next few days meals. I don't plan on putting in a large garden, just some green beans, corn, onions, carrots and probably tomatoes and potatoes. But it would help out on how much we have to buy at the Mercantile each week." Leah told him.

"Don't we know it! Annalise always puts in a garden for us, but as round as she is, she can't bend over to get it planted. We're going to miss all those vegetables this winter, let me tell you!" Andy told her, "Course, I wouldn't trade this baby for anything, garden included!"

"Andy, if you have the seeds and your garden dug up, I see no reason why I can't plant your garden for you and keep it weeded until Annalise is up to doing it." Leah volunteered.

"Leah that would be wonderful!" Andy exclaimed and hugged his little wife, "I'll tell you what. You get that garden planted, and I'll build counters, shelves and tubs and sinks for free. I'll just charge Graham for the lumber, hose, barrel, and tin. You'll save some money and so will I on all those vegetables my wife cans and puts up each summer."

"It's a deal! Now I'd better get started on the curtains and then I'll tackle the garden. It looks to be a busy day for all of us! Annalise are you going to be all right with me working in the garden most of today and not being in the shop with you? I don't mind taking home some of the items to sew each night to get you caught up." Leah told her.

"Getting the garden in will take a load off my mind, Leah! I'll manage as best as I can, I've been doing it up until now, I don't see where doing it a few more days will hurt! It sounds like a win-win situation for all of us!" Annalise leaned over to give Leah a hug and then started sewing on the days accumulation of work to be done. Leah started on her curtains humming, and Andy left to go get lumber and everything else he needed to work at Graham's. It looked like it was going to be a very productive day.

Things hadn't gone the way Charlie had thought they would. The four rooms looked a lot better than they did the night before, but she found out the food from the eatery across the street was horrible! The biscuits were hard as rocks, the gravy lumpy, and chicken raw. Charlie would not eat that slop another day! She didn't want to, but she could cook better than that! She just needed the right supplies. Unfortunately, Jonah didn't see it like she did.

She could still hear him ranting and raving! "I want you to be comfortable up here, but you do realize that you will be helping me in the store most of every day. When are you going to find the time to cook along with everything else? I don't want to drag supplies up here and then be left with a big mess when you're gone! Just cool your horses, princess, and do what you have to do to get by. I agree you need curtains, so you can have your privacy. I don't agree you need another couch because you don't like the one you have!" Jonah had told her firmly. "This is a temporary situation, nothing more, nothing less." With that, he had stormed out the door. Charlie had fumed the entire night. His bed was lumpy, and everything was musty. The sheets, blankets, quilts just had to be washed! Now how am I going to get that done, Charlie thought to herself. I see no clothes lines, nor enough bushes to lay them on when I'm done washing. She made it a point to ask Jonah about it first thing in the morning.

She dressed carefully the next morning. She hated the pillows making her look fat, and the plain hair style and glasses that made her look plain. The last thing she did was put on one of Jonah's aprons over her dress. It was large enough that it hid the ugly color of the dress, kind of! Then she went down the stairs to the store to begin work.

Jonah met her at the stairs. "Today, I just want you to dust shelves and keep things as neat and tidy as you can. By cleaning the shelves, you'll acquaint yourself with the merchandise we have in the store. If there's something a customer wants, you'll know where to go for it. I'll take care of totaling up what they owe and either getting the cash or putting it on their tab." He paused, "I haven't forgot you need something to cover the windows with, you can pick that out sometime today. I'm pretty sure that Annalise has a sewing machine that will get them done pretty quickly. You can get it ready and as soon as I see Andy or Graham, they'll take it over to them."

"Why can't I just run it over to them now?" Lottie asked.

"Because until I know who is and who is not in town, you won't be going anywhere but here in the store and upstairs." Jonah told her firmly. Lottie nodded but she didn't like it. Here she was finally in town, but virtually a prisoner! She wanted to walk up and down the boardwalk and look into all the stores and see what they had to offer. Belligerently, she started dusting and straightening shelves. There didn't seem to be any rhyme or reason to where the items were in the store. Lottie thought if they had women's clothing for instance it should all be in the same section of the store. All the men's clothing should be together, all the bolts of cloth should be together, and on and on! Lottie thought why put it back in the same disorganized way? If she were going to clean this place, she might as well do it right. She wouldn't even ask Jonah about it, he would just yell at her some more! I'll show him, she thought, just you wait and see how organized I can make this store!

Several hours later, Lottie was tired, dirty, and discouraged. No sooner had she cleared off a shelf for items, then she had to find a place for the items she had taken down from the previous shelf. Several times Jonah had asked her where she had put this or that as he helped a customer find what they needed. He always introduced her as his new clerk, Lottie Bell. Lottie would nod her head and smile and then get back to work. By lunchtime, Jonah finally asked her what in the Hell she was doing?

"Jonah, I'm trying to amaze you with my organizational skills. I was trying to put all the women's things together, the men's things together, kitchen items, tools, and so forth. But it's been overwhelming! I finally get a shelf looking good, and then I have to find a place for everything I took off the shelf in the first place!" Her voice started out strong and got weaker as she continued, "I think I've made a mess of everything. Are you going to fire me on my first day?"

"If I could, I probably would!" Jonah threaded his fingers through his hair and looked just as discouraged as Lottie did. "Look, it's a good idea. But there's just so much merchandise in the store that we would have to sort and then start putting it all back on the right shelves. We'd have to do it at night after the customers are all gone. Even then with both of us working, it would probably take all night to get it done right! And after working all day, all night, we'd have to greet customers the next day without getting any sleep. I don't know if it's worth it, Lottie."

"What if we got some help with it?" Lottie asked hopefully. "Do you think that Leah and Graham would help us out for an evening? Do you have any other friends in town that might be willing to help? With more hands it shouldn't take as long as you might think!"

"I'll give it some thought and ask around. I'm not making any promises, but we'll see. I will admit it should make finding what I want easier." With that he went back to helping customers and Lottie went back to straightening and cleaning shelves. At least he didn't yell at her!

CHAPTER 10

Leah finished the curtains and the altering of the dresses. Then she tackled the garden. Leah loved working in the dirt planting seeds and making tiny furrows in the dark brown earth. She hummed as she worked. She knew she probably looked terrible with dirty patches on her dress where her knees had dragged along the ground. Annalise called her in to rest and eat her lunch. Leah was glad for a break. She was pretty proud of what she had accomplished all the same.

Annalise was thrilled at how much she saw done in her garden. At the rate she was planting, she might even finish everything today except for the potato hills. While they ate, they talked over what Annalise had to get done and in what order it needed to be done. It was decided that Leah would take three dresses home with her tonight to put the hems in, the rest they would do tomorrow. Leah went back to planting the garden, already thinking about her own. It felt good to be doing work she was proud of. Cleaning the saloon was honest work, but the atmosphere was nothing short of dismal and gloomy. She also gained the reputation of being a saloon girl even if she never took anyone upstairs or to her room in the back of the saloon. Names hurt, especially when they weren't deserved. Leah vowed that here in Trinity she would keep her good name and that of Graham's. Thinking of him made Leah smile all over again. She was finding herself enjoying being in the presence of a male again. After Keifer, she didn't trust men any further than she could see them. Graham was different, very different. She liked the idea of making a home for him where before he only had a house with a bed. By the end of the day, Leah's back hurt from planting all day, but she had finished everything up except for the potato hills.

"I'll get Andy to put the hills in tonight while I'm making dinner, Leah. Consider the garden done until you have to start weeding it at least! Thank you so much for putting it in, it will make all the difference in our budget this summer and especially this winter in buying supplies! You have already been a lifesaver! Are you sure you don't mind taking those dresses home and putting in the hems?" Annalise asked her, already worried she was asking too much from her employee.

"They need to be done to be picked up tomorrow, after I hang the curtains and put away all the food and dishes, I'll start dinner and work on the hems while it cooks. It's better to be ahead as we begin the day than trying to catch up!" Leah told her trying to convince her that she wasn't working her too hard.

Just then Annalise saw Andy coming up the sidewalk ready to walk Leah home, "Honey, you need to go in and lie down for a while to keep the swelling in your feet down. I'll be back as soon as Graham comes home." Andy kissed Annalise and walked beside Leah. He even offered to help her carry some of the curtains or dresses she was holding.

"I've got it, I think!" She laughed, "Do you mind if after we drop all this off at the house before we go to the Mercantile for a few items? I want to get our seeds for our garden and get meat for tonight's dinner."

"Not a problem," Andy told her. Leah noticed that his eyes were never still. He knew what was going on around them without making it look like he was.

Jonah greeted them as they came in the door and helped her find all the seeds she wanted, and to cut them a nice sized roast. Leah also added a dozen eggs and a bowl of butter and some clothes pins. She waved at Lottie across the store and Lottie waved back. Wondering why Leah could walk up the boardwalk and not her. She did notice that she was being escorted by somebody, but then so could she! Jonah was just being mean! He liked being the boss and telling her and everyone else what to do!

They were only in the store a total of ten minutes, but during that time Lottie stewed and got madder and madder at the situation. As soon as they left, and the store was empty, she erupted. "Why is she allowed to walk up and down the sidewalk and I can't? She even got to go shopping while all I get to do is work in this dirty old store!" Hands on her hips, she yelled at Jonah, forgetting that he was her boss for the time being.

"Look, princess, I'm getting pretty tired of you second guessing me every time I tell you to do something or not to do something! Leah, in case you've forgotten, is now married to Graham. They're making his house into a home just like all newlyweds do. They're trying not to draw too much attention to their situation, but it would look pretty suspicious if she didn't buy meat, and other consumables just like everybody else. Andy stays with her when Graham is at work. He's married to Annalise; the woman Leah works for. It's pretty convenient. In case you haven't noticed, I am not enjoying being your boss or your jailor! You are a royal pain in my ass! I've never seen a woman complain so much or want everything that she can't have! I sure pity the man who finally takes you to wife, you will drive him crazy and he'll never have another sane moment for the rest of his life! Now get back to work, we don't close our doors until eight o'clock tonight!"

Lottie fumed, "Did you at least give the curtains to Andy to give to his wife so that I can have some privacy?"

"As a matter of fact, I did. Leah told me, she would send them over to you first thing in the morning. It looks like you'll have to use the dresses for another night if you want privacy." Jonah told her and then turned to start putting containers away that held the eggs and butter he had measured out to Leah.

Lottie thought the day would never end, but she wasn't looking forward to eating another awful meal from the café across the street. *Why won't Jonah let me cook us something edible for a change!*

Leah started cooking slices of the beef into her skillet and chopping up onions to put in with it. She parboiled some potatoes and even cut up a couple of carrots to cook and serve with the meal. The house smelled good with the bread from this morning and the beef cooking on the stove. She loved the shelves and the kitchen counter. Andy was working on getting her the drainage she wanted from the large tub he had rolled into the corner of the kitchen. Putting away all the supplies she had bought the night before was fun and her idea of having the shelves be deep enough to hold the wooden crates was a good one. She just had to slide out what she wanted and slide it back in. No mess and no fuss!

Putting things away on the shelves under the sink finished getting rid of the clutter in the kitchen. Leah checked on dinner and then went outside to get the clean clothes off the line. She folded some of them and hung the rest up on the nails that Graham had put up last night.

Then she started hanging up the curtains she had hemmed today at Annalise's. It looked like an entirely different house then the one she had entered last night.

She hoped that Graham liked it as much as she did. She felt like she had come home after a long lengthy absence. It was a good feeling. She grabbed Graham's hammer and hung a blanket in front of the large tub for more privacy. She even put one of the empty crates in to put a lamp on and to put some towels under it. Lastly, she put a bar of soap on the top next to the lamp. After planting all day, Leah couldn't wait to try it out tonight!

She sat down in one of the rockers and started sewing on the dresses Annalise needed tomorrow morning. She was content for the first time in a very long time.

Things were going well in the valley. Having Dani or Jo in their homes was pleasant and they were a huge help to two women who had their hands full taking care of babies and gardens and everything else that went into making a home in Montana. Last year, Molly had used the deer skins they had accumulated over the spring and summer to make deer skin pants and shirts for Bo, Rusty, and Red. Molly planned on doing the same thing this year, but she was going to add an additional pair of deer skins for Boone. Making the deer skin pliable enough to sew into clothes was a lot of work. She and Rusty worked together getting the skins ready. She felt like she had a two-week opportunity from getting the garden planted before she started weeding it and picking berries. She thought that with Jo helping her they might not need Rusty, freeing him up to helping their own ranch and that of the Bellamy's.

Jo loved staying at the Callahan's. She loved playing with the babies and helping Molly was fun, too. It still gave her a lot of time to roam the woods like she loved to do. That's what she was doing this morning. She was almost silent as she walked through the tall grass and climbed several trees to get a better view of the spectacular land. Never had she looked at any mountains so close. Molly had told her they could watch the snow on the mountains and know when winter would come as the snow came further and further down the snow-capped peaks against a blue sky. As Jo walked, she picked wild flowers to take back to Molly. She thought about Charlie and hoped that everything was working out well. And then she came to an abrupt stop. Standing before her was an Indian! She wasn't afraid of him, instead she was drawn to him. He wasn't a man, but a very tall boy. His hair was shiny and black and tied in two braids that fell on either side of his face. His chest was bare, he wore only buckskin leggings and moccasins. His bronze colored face was expressionless as he stared at her in return. He was certainly a handsome boy, Jo thought as she watched his black eyes roam over her just as thoroughly as she was doing to him. Suddenly Jo smiled.

Never had Wolf seen anyone like the girl standing before him. Her white hair was magnificent blowing free in the wind behind her. She was slim, looking almost frail, but unlike most white women, her face was a golden tan from spending so many hours in the sun. She seemed to walk on springs as she floated over the tall grass. He was drawn to her, which made him frown. He was done with living in the white-man's world. He had found peace living with his Sioux brothers, adopted mother and father. He was finally accepted for himself, not for what he looked like.

It was Jo who finally spoke first, "Hello! Do you speak any English?"

Wolf didn't speak but nodded.

"Oh, good!" Jo told him in a very pleasant voice. "You are the very first Indian I've ever seen, and you are exactly what I expected to have you look like but you're different, too. I expected to be very frightened of Indians, but you don't scare me. You intrigue me. I get this feeling that we've met before and that we're going to be friends. Do you get that feeling, too?"

Wolf slowly nodded again. But this time he stepped forward and gently touched her hair. It was silky and soft. "You have hair the color of clouds, white girl!"

"What is your name?" Jo asked softly.

"They call me Wolf," He stated proudly. "The Sioux would call you Skah. It means white, because of your hair."

Jo laughed, and Wolf was mesmerized by the soft sounds. "Well, they can call me whatever they want to, but the rest of the valley calls me Jo, it's short for Josephine. What brings you to our valley?"

"Rusty send word to Boone that they need the help of my brothers to keep them safe. My father, Chief, and other braves come to see what their white brothers want from us. I come to see my white mother, Molly Callahan." Wolf told her watching her to judge her reaction.

"That's wonderful, I'm living with the Callahan's until the bad men following us are gone. I'm sure that Molly, Rusty, and Bo will explain it all to your family and friends. I'd better go tell Molly you're here." With that Jo turned and ran swiftly into the woods. All you could see of her was the white hair flitting from tree to tree. Wolf watched her for a few seconds and then he, too, turned and went to tell his Indian family what he had just seen. He was looking forward to seeing 'Jo' Skah again.

Molly was excited to hear that Wolf and his Indian family was coming. They could certainly use their help in keeping the Bellamy family safe in the days, weeks, or even months that passed before they arrived and were apprehended. She knew that Rusty, Bo, Tate and Miller wouldn't rest until this Keifer man was caught and brought to justice. What he had done to Lela was awful, and it sounded like he had done it to a lot of young girls. She was confident that her men could handle them, but to have some extra eyes watching out for them when there was so much to do to prepare for winter, would certainly be good.

Molly started making an extra-large batch of ham and beans and cornbread. She didn't know if she would be feeding Boone and some of the Indians or just Boone and Wolf. She was happy, she missed the cantankerous little man she had found in the woods more than a year ago wounded and very bad shape. When she set about making him better, he had complained the entire time. He didn't know how to talk to anyone without complaining! But he had a heart of gold, and Molly loved him. She knew that he also cared about her and the other inhabitants here in the valley.

When Boone and the other braves arrived at her back door almost an hour later, Boone wasn't feeling so good. He'd had a pain in his side that had started about half way here. It didn't let up or get any better. Now he was feeling like he was going to throw up, and that made the little man angry. You travel pert near fifty miles to see the little lady and by the time he was here, he felt like he was going to have need of her nursing skills again! As the group pulled up into the Callahan's yard, Boone grabbed his side again and promptly fell off his mule. Bo was at his side in minutes and lifted the moaning Boone into his arms. "Molly!" Bo yelled, "We've got trouble. Something is wrong with Boone!"

Molly was out the door as quick as she could and looked with growing concern at the pale and clammy skin of the man in Bo's arms. "Bring him in and put him on the table, let me see what the problem is..." But deep down she already thought she knew what was

126

wrong. The way that Boone was holding his side and moaning, usually meant stomach fever, or rather a bad appendicitis attack. He would need a doctor then, she didn't do surgery. Taking out bullets, putting in stitches, delivering babies, but not anything as complicated as removing an appendix! "Wolf ride hard and get Red! I fear that Boone is going to need the doctor in town, and Red will have to ride hard and fast to get him and bring him here before it's too late!" Her practiced hands moved over the almost unconscious Boone. As soon as she put any pressure on his lower abdomen, he cried out in pain. She looked up at Bo with tears in her eyes, "I can't help him! He needs an operation, and it must be done quickly before his appendix breaks and spreads poison throughout his body." She paused to gain her composure, "All we can do now is pray that Red gets back here in time with the doctor to save his life..." She started doing whatever she could to ease Boone's discomfort. She took off his pants and shirt and covered him with a sheet and a blanket. She put a small bucket for him to throw up in, and she washed him from head to feet. She put on boiling water to sterilize any instruments the doctor might have with him. She tore up an old sheet into bandages, took care of her babies, and continued to pray for Red's quick return.

Red had never been more frightened, not in the war, not even when they were held at gunpoint last year by Anthony's Piderro's men. Rusty and Boone were like fathers to him, he wasn't going to lose one of them if he had anything to say about it!

Luck was on their side, he wasn't even to town when he met up with the doctor coming back from delivering a baby to a woman a few miles outside of town.

"Doc! Doc, hold up!" Red called out at the little man in the buggy. He all but threw himself in front of the doctor's buggy to get it to halt quicker.

"Boy, you know that's a good way to get yourself killed!" Doctor Harris yelled at him. "What would ever make you do such a damn fool thing in the first place?"

"We need your help, and Molly says we need it in a hurry. Boone has stomach fever, and she says you're the only one who can operate on him to save him! I rode like the devil was chasing me to get to you in time!" Red paused even while turning around the buggy. "Will you follow me out to the ranch?"

"Of course, I will. But I can't go as fast as you, nor do I want to. I will go as fast as I can safely make it there. It won't do Boone any good for us to get killed in the process of getting him help!" Doctor Harris used the small whip he carried on the horse and he followed Red out to the valley. Doctor Harris prayed that he would be in time.

Boone had emptied his stomach more times than he could count. There just wasn't nothing left in there but this God-awful smelling stuff. Boone felt like he was going to die, and right now that sounded like a real good idea. At least he'd be free of the pain. Never had he experienced anything that made him double over in pain that seemed to tear his insides apart. He saw what looked to be tears in Molly's face as she labored over him endlessly trying to give him some comfort. He loved the smart and sassy girl. He didn't want her to see him like this. "Molly, for God's sake, give me back my clothes and let me go die in private! A man wants a little privacy at a time like this..." He moaned even as he tried to get up.

"Boone, you are the most aggravating man I've ever met! If you don't quit trying to get up and leave, I'm going to tie you to the table! And another thing, I'm not going to let you die!" Molly yelled right back at him, "You're too onery to die! Nor will I let you die without doing everything in my power to keep you alive! Now unless you want me to put you out with chloroform and do the operation myself, you need to stop fighting me and let me do my job!" Even as she pushed his weak arms back down to the table, Bo ran into the kitchen.

"Red found the Doc on his way back to town, he's right behind him!" Bo informed her.

"Oh, thank God! Catching him half way to town, may give us the time we need to save his life...Bo go take care of his horse and buggy and direct him where to come...Would you ask Jo to come in and watch the boys while I help the doctor operate?" Molly was thinking ahead of everything the doctor would need to start the operation.

Bo didn't answer her, he called for Jo and asked her to go help Molly with the boys while they operated on the Boone, he explained to Wolf what they were going to do. He also thanked him and his brothers for coming. As soon as they got the doctor in to Molly and Boone, he would tell them what was going on. Wolf nodded, and he and his friends got off of their ponies and walked them over to give them water and to let them eat grass while they waited on Boone's operation.

Red didn't stop there, he high-tailed it over to spread the news that the Indians were there to help, and that Boone was in a bad way and was getting an operation by the town doctor and Molly. As soon as Rusty heard, he hurried over to do what ever he could to help his friend.

Doctor Harris didn't even introduce himself. He saw the man on the table and took in everything that Molly had done in preparation of his arrival. He nodded and immediately put his instruments into the boiling water and started washing his hands with the warm water on the counter. His first words to Molly were, "Get washed up girl, I'm going to need help if we're going to get to him in time!"

Molly didn't need to be told twice, she was washing even as he finished. They were in a race against time to save his life. Molly and Doctor Harris worked well together. She knew what instrument he needed even before he asked for it. Boone was finally free of pain as they administered the chloroform to put him out. Molly breathed a sigh of relief that he could finally rest. It took the doctor and Molly over two hours to take the diseased organ out, get him cleaned and stitched up, and resting quietly on a pallet before the fireplace. Then they worked together to clean up her kitchen from having been used as an operating room instead.

Molly called all the braves, Bo, Rusty, and Jo in to eat ham and beans while Boone was still sleeping. The doctor told her he hadn't eaten since early yesterday morning when he had been called out to help deliver a baby the midwife was having trouble with. He was delighted to sit down with the young lady who had been instrumental in saving the old man's life. He was intrigued at eating with the Indians. Never in all his days had he been this close to the savages that held the settlers usually in terror. But here they acted like they did it all the time!

Molly fed her two very hungry babies and put them down for a nap and then joined the others at the table. Rusty was explaining to Wolf why they asked for his friend's help. Wolf would translate to his Indian brothers. Jo's eyes hardly ever left Wolf's face.

She was drawn to this young man. Often in her twelve years, she could sense things were to happen even before they did. Her mother called them premonitions. She also told her, that her grandmother also had the gift. Jo didn't know if she would call it a gift, but she was grateful for it when it saved the life of a neighboring child who was caught in the river when it flooded early one spring. She was the one who told them where to find the missing child. She knew her father was sick long before he started losing weight. She knew there was danger for Charlie, she had felt it every time Charlie would sneak away to meet Keifer. She could feel the evil emanating from the man whenever he or his men were near. Just like she could feel the evil from Keifer, she could feel safe around the Indians, especially Wolf. She knew in her heart that someday; this man would become her mate. She just had to be patient and grow up.She smiled at each of the braves around the table, each of them was a little in awe of her because of her platinum hair. Never had they seen anyone with hair like a white cloud. Skah was a fitting name for the young girl.

CHAPTER 11

Graham and Leah were thrilled with the changes that Andy accomplished that day. Graham couldn't imagine being able to take hot baths any time he wanted to and then just pulling the plug! It was ingenious, he also liked the sink being able to drain as well. He loved the cozy kitchen that Leah had gotten. Watching her working at the hot stove or on the long kitchen counter, made him feel that his house was finally a home. He approved of the curtains she had made, and they still let in the sunlight, but gave them privacy from prying eyes.

They sat down to eat dinner. The meat was tender from simmering so long, the mashed potatoes weren't lumpy, and the bread...was heavenly after just eating the café's food for so long. "How do you make such delicious food after you've been working all day? Andy was singing your praises on planting their garden today. He says it will make all the difference in the world this fall and winter in their budget and in eating so well all year long." Graham told her as he ate.

"Thank you, Graham. I've enjoyed making this house into a home you can be proud of. I love helping out Annalise and Andy. I always liked putting in a garden back home. I hope you don't mind but I bought seeds for here too. Our garden won't be as big or as elaborate as Annalise's, but it should provide for vegetables for us through the summer, and if we're still here, I plan on canning the excess, so you will have lots of food for this winter, too." Leah told him smiling.

"As good as you've got this place looking, and as good as you cook, I just might have to give serious thought about keeping you around permanently!" He teased. But even then, in the back of his mind was the thought that having Leah around all the time wouldn't be bad at all.

"I saw Lottie at the mercantile today. She was cleaning shelves, I think. I didn't get a chance to talk to her, but I did wave at her. Do you think we could go visit them sometime soon?"

"Well, it's strange that you should ask. Andy told me that Jonah asked him if we could go over there one night and help them reorganize the store. It seems that Lottie came up with the idea of putting all the ladies' things together, and the men's, and so forth. They can't do it with customers coming in all the time, so it has to be after they close up at around eight o'clock. He figures with us and the Renosso's and he and Lottie, we should be able to get it done in about four hours. What do you think? Are you up to helping them out tomorrow or the next day?" he asked.

"I'd love too! I think it would be fun, and I know that Lottie would love to meet Annalise. Just seeing Jonah all day and working can't be much fun for her. If rearranging the store will make her happy, then I'll do it!" Leah laughed, "How is Jonah...getting along with

Lottie? I remember she wasn't being very cooperative in the wagon getting here."

"From what Andy told me, she's fighting him every step of the way. But she's met her match in Jonah. Once he makes up his mind to do something, it gets done. He agreed to help out with Lottie for capturing Keifer, and no matter what it takes, he'll keep her safe. Jonah remembers Keifer from the war as well as Andy and I do. We all have a bone to pick with the man, some of us more than others. But the bottom line is, he needs to be stopped one way or another to pay for all the pain he's caused to people over the years." Graham told Leah. She watched his face as he talked about Keifer. His eyes shot sparks off, of one thing Leah was sure, Keifer was going to get what he deserved.

"I'd like to plant our garden tomorrow night after Andy and I come home. While I do up the dishes and sew on some dresses for Annalise, do you think you could dig up the garden area in the back yard? I'll help you if you want me to, but I think we only have one hoe."

"You've got enough to do, I'm going to check if any of our neighbor's have a hand plow I can borrow. It'll be much faster." Graham rose, kissed Leah on the cheek, and walked out the back door to go get a plow.

Leah washed the dishes, cleaned up the kitchen and started sewing. She also started heating up water for both of them to take a bath tonight. Already she was thinking of what to fix tomorrow for dinner and of making curtains to hide the shelves underneath the kitchen cabinet. I wonder if Annalise has any left-over material from making all those dresses that she wants to get rid of. I could make up some rag rugs or start making up a patchwork quilt with all the odd pieces. What else could I do to make this house warmer and cozier? In the back of her mind she remembered that Graham said that he might want to keep her around. She couldn't imagine being able to live with Graham for the rest of her life, it would be heaven on earth.

Two days later found them with her garden put in, curtains on the counter, and she had even found the time to start making some rag rugs. She and Graham were walking over to the mercantile to help them rearrange the store. Andy and Annalise were going to join them, but Andy already told them that Annalise had to have jobs where she could sit down and get off her feet. Jonah told him that would be no problem.

Lottie was beside herself, they were finally going to do something about the mess in the mercantile. Lottie couldn't find anything when she wanted to. She was still having to eat the god-awful food from the café' across the street, and she and Jonah could hardly talk to each other without raising their voices. Tonight, would be the first time since they arrived, that she would actually be able to talk with someone else! She couldn't wait to talk to Lela or Leah. Jonah warned her that she couldn't let it slip what her name used to be. One slip could be all Keifer's men needed to realize where they were being kept.

Jonah had let Lottie hang sheets over his front window to give them some privacy from prying eyes. She wanted it to be a complete surprise when the customers came into the store tomorrow morning. Lottie couldn't wait. She had so many ideas of how to make the store into a better shopping experience, Jonah was rather set in his ways. He told her 'No!' every time she opened up her mouth to suggest anything! He was going to love the reorganized store, he or she would be able to find whatever they wanted in half the time. When he saw how good this worked, she was going to organize the storage room. It was in even worse shape than the store was!

As the four young people came in the door, Jonah handed them aprons to help keep them cleaner moving stuff in the store. He let Lottie tell them how she wanted it done and then they started taking things off the shelves, so they could be moved. The men were in charge of the heavy lifting, the women were in charge of sorting out all the merchandise and putting it in the correct place. Annalise was given the job of sorting all the yarn into same color slots. Lottie had found some smaller sized buckets that could sit on the shelves. Women just had to grab how many hanks of yarn they wanted in the colors they wanted. Annalise was thrilled to get out of the house for a while and still be able to be helpful. Lottie told her when she was done with the yarn, they still had to sort through the thread, and the seed packets. Happily, Annalise went to work.

Lottie and Leah started sorting out everything they had taken off the shelves. Lottie had made up papers for where each of the corners would go. She had a place to put women's, men's, children's, kitchen items, farming items, garden supplies, school needs and books, sewing supplies and bolts of material, and food stuff. Leah and Lottie talked non-stop while they worked. The men could tell they had been friends for years. They both understood the other so well, they often finished each other's sentences. They made a very good team, plus Leah made sure to include Annalise in their discussions so she wouldn't feel left out.

After all the shelves had been moved into the place that Lottie wanted them, the men started sorting through the huge piles of merchandise and Leah and Lottie started putting it on the shelves in an attractive manner. Lottie took several hangers and hung up a couple of the dresses they had for women. She nailed in a few nails and they had to admit it did look nice with the dresses hanging near all the stacks of women's items. She did the same thing for the men and the children's corner. She told them that people could tell with a look where to find what they needed without asking them constantly.

By ten o'clock, Andy told them he was taking Annalise home. She needed her rest, he told them he would return to help them finish. Leah and Lottie both hugged her as she left. A new friendship was formed between the three women. When they were gone talk turned to how things were going at Graham and Leah's. Much to Leah's surprise, Graham started raving about what their home looked like and how good a cook she was!

"I'm telling you, Jonah, after eating the Café' food for so long, the difference is amazing! Every night I come home to a delicious dinner and the smells coming from that old cook stove make my mouth water just thinking about it! We'll have to have the two of you over for dinner just, so you can taste how good a cook Leah is. I get biscuits and gravy and pancakes for breakfast, and then she makes me sandwiches on the best tasting bread I've ever eaten." Graham told them all and winked at Leah's pink face at the praise. "I only had a bed in each of the two bedrooms, she had me throwing out the old lumpy mattress and giving me new ones with sheets filled with fresh cut grass. I've never slept so well, let me tell you. We've got curtains up and we had Andy come over and put in some kitchen counters and shelves, and he made shelves that Leah just pulls out the wooden crates we got from here. In those crates, she keeps her potatoes, onions, carrots, sweet potatoes, flour, sugar, and I don't know what all. Everything else is stacked on the shelves above the three sliding shelves. We picked up two rockers and a table and four chairs at the resale shop, along with dishes and pots and pans and silverware. It saved me a bundle.

Then we came here and got the rest. I don't know how she does it, but Leah works all day long and I still come home to clean clothes, great food, a garden she's already planted, and now she's working on something she calls rag rugs, so we won't have to step on the cold floor first thing in the morning. I have never lived so well!"

"It sounds amazing, that's for sure. Leah has done well adjusting to living with you and working at the Renosso's pretty well. Anyone seeing you would actually think that you were newlyweds!" Jonah told him smiling at Leah and Graham.

"How are things going here? Are you letting Lottie cook and all like my Leah does?"

Lottie had been silent for long enough, she had certainly heard enough about how well things were going for friend and envied her the easy relationship she had with Graham. She actually looks happy, Lottie thought. "No, he does not let me cook! We have to eat the slop they sell at the café! I tried to talk him into letting me cook, but to do that there have to be some major changes is the rooms above us. He doesn't want to be left with a mess when all this is over. He doesn't realize that I would be making it better for him to actually live in the rooms above instead of just sleeping there!"

Lottie was steaming and didn't care who knew it. Leah just looked at Graham and Graham looked at Leah, thanking his lucky stars that he got Leah while Jonah got stuck with the hellion. Jonah stared at Lottie like he wanted to throttle her! Everything that Graham had told him about the house that became a home with Leah sounded good to Jonah but letting Lottie loose to start changing his home was another thing. She was bound to be a loose cannon he didn't want to have to contend with!

Andy arrived back then after taking Annalise back home, "What's going on?" He questioned into the taunt atmosphere.

"Graham was telling us how nice his home is now that you did some work for them and Leah used her magic to make it into a warm and cozy nest for them." Jonah paused, "Lottie was complaining that I won't let her do that to the rooms upstairs. She doesn't realize the work involved into making the counter and the shelves and the mattresses. Not to mention she wants to cover that couch in the parlor, no telling what it would look like by the time she was done! I'm not made of money, and I just don't have a lot of time to spend on fixing up the rooms upstairs, especially when I don't spend any time up there!"

"It really didn't take a lot of money, Jonah." Andy offered, "Just the lumber and time. But if you're worried about the money, hell, I'll throw in my labor to buy some supplies that Annalise would like to get for the baby. You know flannel, yarn, baby powder, and stuff. You could do like Graham and Leah did and go shopping at the resale shop for dishes and such. It shouldn't cost too much. Then just carry up the supplies she needs to

141

start cooking. You would save a lot by just not going over to the café three times a day. She's got to cook better then they do. I'm not telling you what to do, but it's worth thinking about."

Jonah was silent while Andy talked, he was watching Lottie. She was excited about being able to make the upstairs rooms into something more livable. He had been thinking about it for a long time. But he never found the time. With Lottie, he had her labor and Andy's just for sending over some baby stuff. If it would get Lottie to stop complaining, it just might be worth it.

"Lottie, if and I mean if, I let Andy build a counter and some shelves for the kitchen, would you be satisfied to go to the resale shop to get some dishes and stuff? I want you to remember that we're trying to spend as little as possible, not as much...would you stop complaining about everything, so I can have a little peace around here?" Jonah asked her. He was not prepared for her answer.

Lottie squealed and threw herself into Jonah's arms and wrapped her arms around his neck and kissed him, really kissed him. She was so happy! She would be able to change those four rooms into something grand! Jonah was poleaxed at how Lottie's kiss went through his body like lightning. He put his arms around Lottie and held her just to keep her from falling, he told himself. But she felt so good in his arms. He could feel her breasts crushed against his chest even through the pillows she still wore. He took her arms from around his neck and set her a little away from him. "I take that's a yes?"

"Yes, yes, a thousand yeses! I will make you proud of the rooms, and I will be mindful of your budget. I will also start cooking for you as soon as it's done, the sooner the better! I don't think I can even look at another meal from the café!" Lottie told him smiling and laughing.

Jonah couldn't stop looking at Lottie, a smiling Lottie and not a scowling one. She is absolutely beautiful, he thought. Now if I can get her to start smiling more and complaining less, I'll be a happy man!

"Andy, how soon can you come over and do some work around here?" Jonah asked.

"How about tomorrow? I'll also bring Annalise along to pick out what she wants from your store for the baby. We'll time it for Leah to come too to get some more meat or whatever she needs from the store. Then I'll take them all back home and come back and finish up for the day. How does that sound?" Andy liked the confused look Jonah had on his face. He was hoping that both of his friends found women like he had in his Annalise. He saw signs of Graham falling for Leah, and this was the first chink in Jonah's armor he had seen with Lottie.

By the time they finished around midnight, Lottie was smiling from ear to ear. The store had been transformed into something less than a bunch of stuff into an organized place to find everything their customers might want. She and Jonah both thanked their friends over and over again for all their work. They certainly wouldn't have been able to do it without them so quickly. Jonah just kept looking at all the little corners his little clerk had made and how welcoming they were to be finding exactly what you wanted. Hopefully it would make his job a lot easier. As Lottie turned to go up the stairs to bed, she murmured to Jonah, "Thanks, Jonah...I appreciate you letting me fix up the store and the rooms upstairs." Jonah nodded his head, tonight was the first time he had ever heard Lottie tell anyone thanks. It was a start.

The next few days went by in a whirlwind of activity. Andy did come and start working on her counter and her shelves. He also talked Jonah into installing a large tub for bathing. He told him about how easy it was to install a hose for letting all the water out without carrying it out bucket by bucket. Lottie seemed to be walking on air. She was pleasant to his customers and loved all the positive comments they made as they walked through his newly organized store. No longer did they have to spend a lot of time trying to find what they wanted, they just went to the right corner and there it was. Jonah thought they were even selling more than was usual at this time of year.

At lunchtime, he put up his sign that they would be back in an hour, and he and Lottie spent some time in the resale shop. Lottie thought it was a gold mine and loved digging through the stacks of dishes and other necessities. Between the two of them, they found everything they needed, and Graham was right, it didn't cost him an arm and a leg. He helped Lottie gather the supplies she needed from the mercantile and carry it upstairs. It was the first time Jonah had seen the rooms with the curtains on them and how clean Lottie had made it. He carried down the old mattress and carried up the new mattress stuffed with fresh cut grass. Lottie was humming as she put away all the items, they bought on the shelves that Andy built. Then she turned to tell Jonah that dinner would be in one hour, if that was all right with him.

"It sounds great, I'll finish up in the store while you cook up some food and finish putting things away." Jonah couldn't get away fast enough. Watching Lottie when she was happy was a habit, he could very well be fast acquiring!

Lottie's cooking was heaven after eating the café's food for the last six years. The smell of baking bread coming down the stairs seemed to linger in the store all day. Lottie was mindful of not spending too much in the store in the way of meat and such, but at this point Jonah didn't mind. He was actually looking forward to eating meals rather than just eating to keep going. He also liked sitting down at the little table to eat a meal with Lottie. It was nice to put the store out of his mind while he ate and talked over the day with her. Her complaining was considerably less, but she still made suggestions that would make things better for them in the long run.

One of them was to buy about a dozen of the little hand baskets that they had over in the resale shop. When his customers came into the mercantile, they could pick up one of the baskets to put their purchases in as they shopped.

Another was to put something in his front window. Lottie suggested painting Jonah's Mercantile or Macdonald's Mercantile on the window and sitting on the window sill would be items from the store that their customers might not know they carried.

Lottie also wrote down every item in every one of the little corners they had made and listed how many they had. All Jonah had to do was look at the list and write down what they were low on and reorder it. It was a great way to take inventory, much simpler than what he had been doing.

Jonah was so impressed how nice the rooms looked upstairs and the mercantile, he gave the go-ahead for all three of her suggestions. That's when she said they needed to organize the storage room. As it was, there could be five large bags of flour in there, but they wouldn't be together, they would be in five different places in the storage room. Lottie wanted to put all the same kind of thing together to make it easier to find what they needed. Jonah didn't know if he was up to another huge upheaval so soon after redoing the rooms and the mercantile, but Lottie was persistent. Together, the two of them could do a little bit every night after they closed up for the night and after they ate supper.

After a week of listening to Lottie try and persuade him to do it, Jonah agreed. As he waited for Lottie to come down to help after doing the dishes, Jonah had to agree that all of her suggestions so far had proved to be worth the time and effort they had put into it. The ladies loved the little baskets. He saw several people start to walk past his store and came back to look in his front window and see something they liked and bought. Her inventory lists saved him time and money by knowing exactly how many of each item they had, before he guessed, and they came back having twice as many of some things and none of others. He also had to agree that eating her cooking rather than the cafés was way better. He had actually kept track of how much they were spending on food from the mercantile, and how much he usually spent at the café. The food was more than paying for itself! Inside Lottie's beautiful head was a good brain and a lot of business sense.

Lottie chose that time to come running down the stairs to help him. She had brought with her a broom to sweep it out as they organized. Jonah did the heavy lifting and made it look easy! Lottie swept after he moved the items and helped lift things off the shelves and wipe them down as well. It was going pretty well, they had half the storage room done. Lottie was standing on a small ladder handing down bags of supplies to Jonah. He was putting them on the floor behind him for lack of a better place. Already the storage room looked better, you could actually walk and not trip over a hundred-pound bag of rice or flour. Lottie was reaching around the ladder and her weight was no longer centered on the ladder when she felt the ladder slip! It was a good thing that Jonah had excellent reflexes, he turned and caught her even as she fell. Lottie slid down Jonah's body gently instead of landing on the hard floor. She looked up just as Jonah looked down to ask if she were all right. It seemed the most natural thing in the world to lower his head and kiss her. Lottie lifted up her arms and they went around Jonah's neck. Never had she been kissed like Jonah was kissing her now! Her entire body felt on fire. She didn't want the kiss to end...ever! Jonah was of much the same mind...never did he think that kissing Lottie would take over his mind and all his good intentions of keeping her safe!

After several kisses and several minutes, Jonah loosened Lottie's hands and arms from around his neck. He took a step back, "I'm...sorry...Lottie, I had no intention of kissing you...It would be a bad idea to get involved with Keifer coming and all. I want to keep my mind on keeping you safe, and not on trying to get you into bed...You and I are too different...It just wouldn't be a good match...It's not you, it's the situation we find ourselves in..." His voice dwindled away. He was still starring at Lottie. He saw her swallow and take a step back.

"I agree...Jonah. The last thing I...we...need right now is an emotional entanglement." She kept her head bowed looking down at her feet as she talked, "I'm tired, how about we finish the storage room tomorrow night?" Without waiting for an answer, Lottie left the room and headed upstairs. She didn't want Jonah to see the tears in her eyes or know how much his words had hurt him.

She had been living in a dream world! Jonah didn't want anything to do with her. She remembered his words of just a day or so ago, telling her how sorry he felt for the man who would end up with her as his wife...She had built all kinds of romantic endings for her after this was all over. Jonah would see how much of a help she was to the store and how different his life was with the upstairs looking so grand and eating such good meals that he never wanted to go back to eating in the café' again! She was just fooling herself, she realized. He was just humoring her to get her to stop complaining. She knew she had been a shrew the first few weeks she had been there. But she could change, she would show him. She just needed time, and they had time waiting for Keifer and his hired guns to show up in town.

Thinking about Keifer made Lottie remember that she was going to get a derringer from the store and start carrying it around in her aprons. If and when, Keifer came to the store, she was going to be ready for him. She might have to save Jonah's life and he could see how brave and courageous she was. Then he'd change his mind about her. She knew she was grasping at straws, but it gave her hope and right now she needed something to hold on to. Hope was all she had!

CHAPTER 12

Boone was healing slowly. He knew he had been very close to death, and he owed his life to Molly and Doctor Harris. He didn't know Harris, he was just an old sawbones from town, but he did know Molly. It was like having a daughter who pampered and kept telling what he could and could not do! They argued like cats and dogs and both of them loved every minute of it!

Chief Enapay's braves were situated all around the valley. If they saw anything to report, they did. Otherwise, you'd never even know they were there. Wolf came to Molly's often. He liked visiting with her and holding the twins. But his major reason was Jo or Skah as the Sioux now called her. They spent a lot of time just roaming the woods near her home. They brought home fish, wild rhubarb, and honey. Jo would rather be romping through the trees with Wolf than anything else in the world, but she also liked helping Molly. At the present, they were preparing deerskins into becoming pliable enough to sew into clothes. Jo had even talked Molly into making her a pair of deer skin pants and a fringed top that would come to almost her knees. Wolf had already made her a pair of moccasins that she wore constantly. Boone had gifted her with a knife in a sheath that she had tied around her waist.

Everyone was so busy in the valley, planting the last of the crops, branding the cattle and new calves and foals, making up more corrals, chopping wood, picking enough berries to keep them all winter, making clothes for growing children and their men, and cooking enough food to keep them all going. Molly loved doing for her family and knew that every woman in the valley felt the same way. Molly made weekly visits on Violet and Miriam to check how their pregnancies were progressing. She also made time to go and visit Willa. Loosing her husband and then all her children at the same time was increasingly hard on the woman. She was working her garden, helping Red with the animals as much as she could, and she mourned them all. She loved the valley and got along well with Red Dalton. Rusty came to visit often bringing with him some meat for the smoke house, or news about the other families in the valley. She loved hearing how Dani was doing with May and Miller and little Gus, and how Jo was doing with Molly, Bo, and the twin boys Joey and Jake. She had never met Boone, but both Red and Rusty loved telling her stories about every encounter they had ever made with the little man. Willa almost expected him to be walking on water when she met him!

She missed Ed so very much. Making a home in the valley was supposed to have been for both of them to enjoy. She did all the things she would have done if Ed had been here and often talked to him in her mind. She didn't feel quite so lonely by doing so.

It was the middle of May when the Indians noticed the first stranger. He didn't come on their land, but he would sit on his horse and watch them all through his telescope. Then he would write down notes in a little black book he carried with him. He never approached any of the men in the valley. He watched every day for nearly two weeks, and then he was gone. One day he was at his camp, and the next there was no sign of him. The people of the valley who were waiting for Keifer Kutter to make an entrance, couldn't for the life of them figure out who the stranger was and what he wanted.

By now, Jo or Skah, had her deer skin leggings and fringed top. She was brown as a berry from so many hours in the sun. The only thing that kept her from looking just like another Indian, was her white hair. She and Wolf had become inseparable. Wolf was teaching her the ways of the Sioux. He taught her how to track down game, and what food in the forests was good to eat. He also taught her how to protect herself. Jo had always been pretty good with a gun, but with a bow and arrow, she was excellent. She often challenged Wolf in competitions. Could she outrun Wolf? Could she throw him over her shoulder in a fight? Could she track him through the forest without being seen? Could she make fire without matches? One of her hardest challenges was whether she could use the skins of the animals they caught and make a teepee with it. It must withstand a strong wind and heavy rains, and the smoke from the fire must go up and disappear when it opened up into the sky. Amazingly, she passed every test that Wolf threw at her. He was very proud of her and hoped one day to make her his woman. He knew that they were both too young to speak such thoughts aloud, but in his heart and in Jo's heart, they shared the same thoughts and wishes.

Jo was running through the forest seeking out Wolf, she had a question to ask him. She was not paying attention to her surroundings when without warning, a hand snaked out and grabbed onto her white braids. Tears came to Jo's eyes at the pain that came to her head from grabbing onto her hair. She turned furious eyes to her assailant. She had never seen him before.

He was dirty and stunk. His jeans were filthy, as was his shirt. When he smiled, he was missing several teeth and his breath almost made her want to throw up. "Well, look at what I found! It's a half Injun, half white girl. What you doing dressed like an Injun? Can you speak any English?" He laughed, "What's the matter, cat got your tongue?"

Jo stared at the young man. She wasn't quite sure how much of a threat he was to her. She still had her knife, but he was several times her weight and height. She watched him carefully to see what his next move would be. For some reason, she wasn't afraid. She knew that if she cried out, Wolf's friends were somewhere in the forest ready to come to her aid.

The young man got tired of waiting and reached out to touch her arm to pull her closer to him. Jo dug in her heels and refused to get any closer to the stranger. Her resistance made the man angry. He pulled harder on her hair and her arm at the same time and threw Jo off her balance. She went flying right into his arms.

"Now see what happens when you don't do what I want you to do!" The stranger laughed, but his eyes didn't register his humor. They were black and seemed bottomless, as if he didn't have a soul. "I think you and me, are going to get to know each other real well before my friends get here. If you're nice to me, maybe I won't share you with all of them...Yes, siree, I think we're going to get along real well. You don't talk too much, so you won't make too much noise and spoil all my fun. I may even think about taking you with me, after we finish our business. How does that sound to you? Would you like for me to buy you a pretty dress or something?" He kept waiting for Jo to answer him or to make some sort of sound. When she didn't, he got braver and braver, by now he had moved his hand from her hair to holding her with both her arms. He was bending down to kiss her when without warning, Jo raised her knee up and hit his privates. Doubling over with pain, the stranger still did not let go of Jo. Instead, he pulled her down with him.

"So, that's the way it's going to be...is it? I was going to try to be nice, but no more, if you like it rough, then rough it will be!" He raised one of his hands and back handed her across the face.

Jo had never been hit before in her life! Her head was spinning, and she saw stars for a few seconds, then she grabbed her knife and went for his throat! Up to that point, she hadn't made any noise at all, but fury made her growl low in her throat as she lunged at him. No one was ever going to hit her like that ever again!

She managed to give him several slices across his chest and his arms before he disarmed her. He was bleeding from a half-dozen cuts and madder than hell that some little-bit of a thing was able to do that much damage in such a short time. He had been gentle up to that point, but no more! He hauled back his fist and slugged her across her jaw. Jo saw black and fainted from the pain that had exploded inside her head.

The stranger took advantage of her unconscious state and quickly had her tunic and leggings off her. He was in the process of undoing his own belt when he felt a thud in his back. Quickly, his arms and hands became heavy and he felt the pain in his back spread over his entire body. Wolf ran forward and withdrew his knife from his back and used it to slit his throat. He tossed the stranger aside as he knelt to care for Jo. He gently touched the darkening bruise on her jaw from where he had hit her. He carefully put her clothes back on her, knowing she would be embarrassed when she woke up and found herself naked in front of him.

Still she did not wake up, he picked her up and started walking towards Molly's cabin. Molly would know what to do and how to care for Jo. Wolf didn't think about the stranger he had left in the woods or what his presence might mean to the rest of the valley. His one and only thought was to take care of his woman.

Two braves saw him coming and what or rather who he was carrying, and they ran forward to help him with his heavy load, but Wolf wouldn't give her up to anyone. He did tell them of the stranger's body back in the woods from thence he had come. "Go, see if you can find out if he's alone or with others who wish to do damage to my friends." Even without an answer, they turned and ran swiftly back to where his body lay.

They were not given the chance to search his body, two others had joined the dead body. They were studying the footprints left in the dirt around the body. "I don't know what happened here, but somebody is going to have to pay for Buck's life with their own! Kutter sent us here to find those girls, and we will, but first we got to follow those tracks and kill the bastard who got the drop on our friend!" The taller of the two men yelled.

"Cool down, Keith. Let me study on this a little bit. Did you notice that Buck's pants were being unbelted?" the shorter man asked. "Either, Buck found himself a female out here and was going to have some fun, or he was getting ready to take a shit. My guess is the first one. Buck was a randy guy, if there was a girl around here, wouldn't matter if she was nine or ninety, he'd be on them like flies on shit."

"You're right, Cody." Keith nodded, "Now that I study on things, look how that grass is matted down almost like someone was lying on it. Nother thing, that knife lying beside Buck's body wasn't his. It's a mite small for a man, but just the right size for a female to have. I'm thinking that Buck was thinking with his pecker and didn't notice when the girl's husband or brother came up from behind him and stopped him from having any more fun ever!"

"I don't know who came up and done him in, but it's his own fault for trying to diddle when we got work to do! I say we get out of here and head for town, before we get the whole valley up in arms. We'll check out the town and come back in a few days to finish checking out the people who live in the valley. We don't have much time to get the bounty that Kutter put on both of those women's heads. I don't want to follow in Buck's footsteps and find myself on the other end of that knife anytime soon." Cody told his friend and they both climbed into their saddles and rode away at a pretty good clip.

Then and only then did Wolf's friends go and pick up Jo's knife and strip the stranger of his own knife and guns. They also took his horse, he sure wouldn't have any more use for it. They headed for Molly's cabin, they knew that that was where Wolf would head to get help for the wounded Jo. Once they found out how Skah was doing, they would send word to the rest of the valley that Kutter's men had been seen.

Molly had Wolf put Jo on the table so she could clean her head wound thoroughly. She sent Wolf to go get Willa, Jo's mother. She knew if any of her boys had gotten hurt, she would want to know. Willa wouldn't be any different than any other mother would be. Jo was still sleeping, Molly worried that she may have a concussion from being hit so hard. She cleaned the abrasions on her face gently and applied cool cloths to her forehead and waited for any change in breathing for her to wake up.

It seemed to take only minutes for Wolf to return with Willa. She was crying silently as she stood over Jo and held her hand. "What happened?" Willa asked the room for she hadn't taken her eyes off her youngest daughter since she came into the room.

"One of three men attacked Jo. She fought him bravely and gave him several cuts on his chest and arms, he got mad and punched her with his fist...He was going to rape her, he had removed her clothes and started on his own when Wolf arrived and stabbed him in his back and then cut his throat...He dressed her and brought her here...Two of the braves with Wolf went back to get the man but by then two others had arrived. They didn't even stop to bury him. They left to go to town to get away from the Indians they were sure that were going to attack them at any moment." Molly told her quietly.

Willa looked up and reached out to grab Wolf's hand, "Thank you Wolf, for saving my daughter...My family owes you and your friends our heartfelt gratitude for saving my Jo. If there's anything we can do for you or the others, just name it and it will be done."

Wolf nodded his head, he couldn't speak. He appreciated all that Jo's mother had said, but until his Skah was awake and well again, he would continue to pray to all the gods of the Sioux and the white man's god as well.

Bo arrived with Rusty and they loaded up Buck's body in the wagon to take to town to see if Lela could identify the man as one of Keifer's. Boone came down the stairs to the loft carefully, grabbed his rifle and went to sit on the front porch to stand guard over his family. Wolf's two friends went into the loft and watched from there. Feeling that Molly would be well taken care of, Bo and Rusty left and promised to hurry back. They sent Red to all the families in the valley to be on the alert for any strangers coming back to get the killed man.

CHAPTER 13

Everything for Leah was wonderful. She loved living with Graham, he was everything she had always wanted in a husband. She knew she was falling in love with the man, but she couldn't seem to stop herself. She already felt the heartbreak she would feel when they captured Keifer and all his men and her marriage would end. Some part of her wanted the charade to go on and on, but she knew Keifer, he didn't have that much patience. Leah just decided to enjoy every day as much as she could and store up all the happy memories for when she had to leave. She knew that she could see their marriage annulled and stay and see Graham all the time, it would just be too painful. Once everything had been taken care of, she would leave and go to one of the other small towns in the Montana Territory and start over. After helping Annalise in her store, Leah felt like she could have her own small shop making clothes for people or curtains, whatever she needed to do.

Lottie wasn't as happy as Leah. Since the night in the storeroom when Jonah kissed her, she and Jonah were pretending that nothing happened. They finished up the storeroom the next night, but Jonah stayed far away from her. They were talking politely to each other instead of yelling, but the strain was there almost as a physical barrier between the two. Lottie loved her living quarters now that they had been made livable. She had even spent each night after dinner with Jonah, covering the hideous couch in the parlor. She had found some dark brown canvas in the storeroom that Jonah was going to throw out. Lottie secretly carried it upstairs to cover the couch. Whenever Jonah came upstairs to eat, he never looked in any of the other rooms. He ate his meal as quickly as possible and left. Lottie had several hours to work on the couch before she became so tired, she could fall asleep. She tried not to dream of Jonah, but she couldn't control her dreams.

Even though Lottie and Jonah weren't talking very much, that didn't stop Lottie from making several more suggestions about the store. Her first was to nail down a yardstick on the counter. It would make it much easier to measure out material if the yardstick was on the counter and the customer could see that they were getting every inch of material they had asked for.

Her second was to put a bell above the door, so they could hear every time a customer came into the store. Lottie didn't want to be caught off guard with Keifer coming into the store or anyone of his gun men.

Her third idea was to put a small board at the entrance of the store so that the men could scrape their shoes off before they entered. Lottie was tired of sweeping up mud every day that was brought in on their feet. Jonah laughed out loud at that suggestion, he just couldn't see their male customers scraping their boots for Lottie or anyone else.

Her last suggestion was that she carry a derringer in her pocket at all times and if Jonah didn't want her carrying a derringer, then she would wear Colts around her waist to feel safe.

Jonah wasn't feeling so chipper either. All he could think about was how good Lottie felt in his arms. He had never been in love before, and the idea of his being in love with the unpredictable Lottie gave him nightmares! He'd never have any peace with her around permanently. But he didn't like the thought of her leaving, she had brought his rather calm and boring existence into life. She made him madder than anyone else could. She also made him laugh more than he had in years. She was a damn good cook, he never wanted to go back to eating at the café across the street, and he liked how cozy the upstairs apartment was with curtains and a tablecloth. And most of all, life with Lottie was never dull. He actually felt young again. But that didn't mean that he had lost all common sense, marrying Lottie would be a disaster...she would make someone a good wife, but he knew that he wasn't that someone.

Jonah finally gave in on three of her four suggestions. He nailed in a yardstick on his counter. He made a bell to sound above the front door, and he allowed her to carry a derringer in her pocket. He hoped that would give him a little peace and quiet for a while, but he wasn't holding out much hope.

Bo and Rusty arrived in town shortly after noon. They immediately went to the Sheriff's office to find Graham. He would know where to find Leah so she could identify the unknown gun man.

Graham and Ren were in the Sheriff's office drinking coffee. Graham was feeling mellow. He loved living with Leah. She was gentle, funny, and hard working. She was beautiful even with that god-awful disguise she had to wear all the time. He couldn't keep her out of his mind, and he didn't try to. He knew he was going to have a heart-to-heart talk with her very soon about making their marriage permanent. He had never been in love before, but he couldn't imagine life in the little house without her. She had crept into his heart and he found that he didn't want her anywhere else. The thought of her leaving him after all this was over and done with, was heart-wrenching. He didn't ever want to let her go.

Graham looked up when he saw Bo and Rusty. "What's up? What's wrong to bring you both into the town?" He was suddenly worried that their peaceful idle was about to come to an end.

"A strange man, a gun man, attacked Jo, Charlie's little sister today in the woods near our home. Wolf attacked the man and killed him. Jo is unconscious at our home. Molly and Willa are with her now. There were two others with the man. They left to come to town. We need to know if the man we found is one of

Keifer's. We'll need Leah to identify him if she can." Bo told him quickly.

"You're right. Follow me to the Renosso's residence and store. Leah works for them during the day sewing. Annalise Renosso is about to give birth to their first child any day now. Follow me and we'll go talk with Leah about possibly identifying the man in the wagon. What do the other two gunmen look like? Do you know?" Graham was talking as he walked toward the end of town.

"Two of Wolf's friends saw them, but they didn't give us anything to go by. Just two white men that both smelled." Rusty told him and laughed. "I'd say that's about half the population of Trinity!"

"You got that right!" Graham told him. "I never knew so many men had such an aversion to bathing. Sometimes the smell alone will knock you out when you go into a saloon to break up a fight. And we hate like hell to bring them back to the jail to stink it up!"

It didn't take any time at all to come to the Milliner's Shop of Annalise. Graham went in and asked if he could talk to Leah for a few minutes outside. Leah got up and followed Graham without saying a word. Graham grabbed her hand as they neared the door. Leah wasn't scared with Graham around, she knew that he would keep her safe no matter what happened. She saw Rusty and Bo on a wagon seat. She also saw a body in the back of the wagon. Her heart stopped, whose body was in the back of the wagon?

"Leah, honey, somebody attacked little Jo. She's going to be fine, but the man was killed. We need to know if you recognize the man as one of Keifer's. Can you do that for us?" Graham asked her softly.

Leah nodded her head, she wanted this nightmare to end, but she didn't know if she was up to looking at a dead man. Graham pulled back the top of the blanket covering the body. Leah took a step back shaking and trembling at the sight of all the blood. She had never seen any dead bodies in all her life and this one had come to a violent end. "His name if Buck...he works for Keifer. He's one of the men he hires when he wants something done and done quick...I poured a pot of hot coffee on his...lap...once when he grabbed me as I worked in the saloon. He never touched me again. But I couldn't forget his face...He usually works with two other men...Keith is tall and thin, and Cody is shorter and broader. I don't know their last names. But they're usually dressed in dark colors and they don't bathe very often. I stayed as far away from them as I could. Does that help?" She looked up at Graham and he nodded his head. "Is Jo going to be all right? Shouldn't Lottie know about her sister? She and Jonah need to know they're in town."

"As soon as I get you settled and alert Andy of their presence, we'll take the body to the undertaker and then tell Jonah and Lottie all about it. She won't be able to go home to see Jo, but it should help put them on their toes to watch out for the two men." He kissed Leah and went with her back into see Annalise as to where they might find Andy at this time of the day.

"Andy should be working for Doctor Harris. The good doctor needed some shelves to put all his supplies on. He was tired of the clutter in his office and in his operating room. Hilde Schultz, the midwife around here, told him she would help him organize it all when she comes over to clean and wash his clothes this week. Why do you need Andy?" Annalise asked suddenly concerned what they needed her husband for.

"Bo and Rusty from down in the valley asked some questions about building that I didn't know anything about. I knew Andy would, we'll probably head over there, and they can get some answers to their questions. Thanks for letting me speak to Leah. You ladies have a good day!" Graham kissed Leah again and squeezed her hand. He whispered in her ear, "Don't leave here without me or Andy!" Leah smiled and nodded. She promised.

Their next stop was to Doctor Harris's office and home. Doctor Harris had a five-room home. Three of the rooms were for his medical practice, he had an examination room, a room for his surgery, and one where he kept all his supplies and extra cots if he needed them for his patients. His home made up the other two rooms, a kitchen and a bedroom.

Hilde Schultz was a middle-aged woman who had managed to raise her children after her husband was killed in the War Between the States. She cooked bread

167

for several of the bachelors in town, cleaned houses and the jail house, and did laundry for several homes in town. Whatever was needed to keep the children fed, dressed, and warm she lent her efforts towards them. All four of her children were grown now and lived within a day's travel. They were all married, and Hilde had helped deliver all of her three grandchildren. She was small and had a thatch of steel-gray hair that was forever coming out of her bun. Her clothes were old and worn, but as clean as she could get them. Her home always smelled good with all the bread she baked, and she was always the first to ask someone down on their luck to come and share her meal with them. She was always on the go and kept herself busy.

She was with Doctor Harris and Andy when the wagon and Graham arrived. "Don't tell me, Annalise is in labor!" Hilde cried out and made to go get her supplies to come help her. Andy paled at her suggestion and made to rise as well.

"Annalise is fine and as of a few minutes ago was not in labor!" Graham quickly told the group at large, "But I do need to talk to Andy about a few things, if I could borrow him outside..."

Andy got up and brushed his pants off, he followed Graham outside. That's when he saw Bo and Rusty and the wagon with the body inside. "Who is it?" He asked.

"We had Leah identify him. He's one of Keifer's boys, he had two others in town. One tall and one short, and they both smell and dress in dark clothes. We wanted to tell you and warn you about them. The guy in the wagon attacked Jo, Charlie's little sister. Their friends, the Indians, found him and killed him. It looks like Jo may have a concussion, but she should be all right. But we wanted to put you on your guard. I know you have Annalise to worry about and the last thing you need is something else to worry about, but I'd rather you be safe than sorry." Graham told him. "We're going to take the body to the undertaker and then go warn Jonah and Charlie. Ren and I plan on walking through town nice and slow to see if we can spot them. Keep Leah at your house until I come for her. I don't want you to be away from Annalise at a time like this, and I don't want Leah to be alone either."

"You got it, Graham. You and Ren be careful, we both know that Keifer only hires low-life's. They'll shoot before they ask questions. Watch your back. I'll watch over the women." He nodded to Bo and Rusty and went back inside to finish the job so he could return home to his wife and Leah.

They dropped off the body and told the undertaker to bury him with the name Buck on the cross. They didn't know his last name and they certainly didn't want to contact Keifer that one of his men were dead, and to ask them what was his name! Then they headed to the Mercantile. They found Lottie painting 'MacDonald's Mercantile' on the front window. It looked really good. She had painted the entire thing in black first and was adding red to look like a shadow behind the letters.

"Looks good, Lottie. I didn't know you were a painter as well as a cook and clerk!" Graham told her as they approached.

"Thanks, Graham. I'm a woman of many talents..." Her voice gave way when she saw Bo and Rusty. "What's wrong? What's happened to my family?"

Jonah appeared at the door of his store, "Gentlemen, why don't you come in. the store is empty right now and it would be a perfect time to find out what's going on. Lottie put down your paints for a few minutes and let's hear what they've got to say."

Graham and Bo ushered Lottie in, Rusty stayed a minute to look at the sign and at the window display. Jonah's store was looking up from what he usually saw, he wondered how much credit could be given to the troublesome Lottie for the changes in the store. Maybe she wasn't the bubble-head she appeared to be. Then Rusty followed them into the store.

Graham didn't waste any time. "Lottie, this morning Jo was attacked by a stranger in the woods near Bo's home. She's unconscious but should recover. Wolf got to her in time and killed the son-of-a-bitch. Leah recognizes the man they found. But he didn't come alone. He always travels with two side-kicks, one tall and one shorter. They always wear dark clothes and they have an aversion to baths. Leah says you should stay downwind of them to keep from smelling them. We wanted to warn you and let you know about Jo."

"Can I go see her?" Lottie asked and looked up at Jonah as she spoke.

"I'm afraid not, Lottie..." Jonah began. He put his arm around Lottie, "It just wouldn't be safe for you to be out right now. I'm sure that Bo and Rusty will keep us informed as to how your little sister is and what's going on in the valley. We need to stay alert and watch out for the two men you mentioned, but I have to tell you if we go by smell, half the miners that come in here smell pretty bad. Lottie suggested that we give away lye soap with each of their orders!"

"Will you tell my mother and sisters that I'm doing well, and...that I miss them a lot? Also tell them that when all this over, I'll be back out to see them as soon as I can." Lottie's voice trembled as she talked. This was not the same young hellion that Rusty had dropped off a little more than a month ago!

"We sure will and we'll keep you updated on how Jo is doing and everyone else. I'll try to send Red in once a week to let you know what's going on in the valley. One of the deputies will ride out and let us know how you are all doing in town. How does that sound?"Rusty assured her patting her hand. He didn't like to see any woman distressed, but one of Willa's was especially hard to accept. "You all take care now, we'll see you soon. By the way, Jonah, your store looks really good. I've never seen so many changes in all my days! I figured you'd never change it as long as you've been here."

"You can thank Lottie for all the changes you see. She's made me see things through her eyes. I fought her tooth and nail, but she won, and to tell you the truth, I'm glad. I like the changes, too! It's all I wanted to happen but didn't know how to go about it. Lottie did. I don't know what she'll have me doing next, but you can bet it'll be something else!" Jonah told Rusty and the men. Lottie couldn't believe her ears, Jonah was giving her praise for all the changes and he liked them. She was thrilled, maybe she wasn't the total disaster he thought she was!

When they left, Jonah went back to the ledgers and Lottie went to finish the sign with a lighter heart than when she started it. She was worried about her sister, but Jonah liked what she was doing! Suddenly the day didn't seem so bad after all.

Graham went and got Ren and together they started quartering the town. They wanted to see who the men were and exactly what they were up against.

Jo didn't wake up for three hours. When she did, she had a horrible headache that made her sick to her stomach and she was seeing two of everything. Molly told them she probably had a concussion. She would need to stay very quiet for a few days, possibly a week or more for the symptoms to disappear completely. Until then, she would give her some sage tea for the inflammation, a little laudanum to help her sleep and help with the pain of the concussion. They would just have to be patient until she recovered. Willa was much relieved that Jo had woken up and understood that she would recover slowly. She hugged her young daughter and then hugged Wolf.

"Thank you again Wolf for saving my daughter. You and your family will always be welcome at our home. If there's ever anything that I can do for you, just let me know. My girls and I will help in any way we can." Willa told a surprised Wolf. He wasn't used to being hugged by white women, only Molly and Jo. He nodded his head, he understood. "And lastly, Molly, I don't know how we will ever repay you for all you've done first with Ed and now with Jo. What would we ever do without you?!" And then she held Molly gently crying over the good news about her daughter.

"No thanks are ever necessary, Willa. We're family here in the valley. We all do whatever we can to help each other, and that includes Wolf's family. You've had to cope with so much these last few months, you've held up very well. First traveling in less than ideal conditions, secondly having Ed so sick, getting set up in a new place, putting in fields, gardens, making your house into a home, and then to lose all your girls to other families. I know it was for their own good, but I also know how much you must miss them. You come visit Jo anytime you can, you will always be welcome, and I know how much Jo misses you and her sisters. She is such a delight! She's always bringing home berries or rhubarb. She loves being there when there's a new baby to be brought into the world, it doesn't seem to matter whether it's piglets, chicks, calves, foals, puppies or kittens! Thank you for loaning us the joy of your daughter!" And then Molly gave Willa a hug. "Wolf would you gently lift Jo up so we can make her a pallet by the fireplace. She'll be warm there and can rest as much as she wants."

Carefully Wolf lifted up Jo, he held her against his heart. As Molly made up a pallet on the floor, Wolf cherished the time he was able to hold his Skah. He would give his life to save hers, he would be her guardian angel. He would always keep her from harm. Even as he put her on the pallet, Jo opened up her eyes and she smiled through her pain at Wolf. She touched his face and whispered, "Thank you, my Wolf. You saved me from certain shame and pain. I...love...you..." And then she closed her eyes and fell asleep. But for Wolf, it was enough.

CHAPTER 14

Graham and Ren did start searching the town for two dirty, smelly gunslingers. They started with the saloons and pleasure houses. The town of Trinity had several of each of these. It seemed that every town west of the Mississippi had at least two or three saloons and at least one pleasure house. Trinity was no different. They considered themselves a clean little town, but they knew that the men outnumbered women ten to one. Those men without women of their own needed a place to let off steam and somewhere to ease their manly needs. They had four saloons and two pleasure houses. They went to the saloons first. First Graham would go in and stand beside the door to get the lay of the land so to speak, and then Ren would follow. Together they would walk slowly up to the bar, looking at every man at the poker tables and every man bellied up to the bar.

All of the saloons and pleasure houses were kept on one end of the town, the Sheriff called it Hell's Acre of Sin. For a few dollars, a man could get a woman to do whatever he wanted her to do and he could get himself drunk as well. Most of the time, they kept disruption to a minimum. The bars all had enormous barkeeps that didn't brook any type of argument or disagreements. The pleasure houses all had muscular men at the door, and they took all guns and knives away from their customers. They didn't want any altercations, and they didn't want any of their girls hurt too badly either.

They checked out Brownie's Bar, Polly's Bar, the Tip Top Saloon, and Sal's Saloon. They didn't see the two men they were seeking. They both knew that they could be in one of the rooms above the bar seeking ease with one of their 'ladies.' But for now, they ruled them out. Then they went to the pleasure houses, Flowers of Delight, and Lil's House of Pleasure. Here they talked to the men at the doors, they would know if anyone matching their description had entered the houses. They each shook their heads, so far, they were striking out. They did warn the men and the barkeeps to keep their guard up and send for the law if the two men showed up. They were trouble and no body wanted to be shut down for causing trouble.

Then they went to the livery. The two men might have checked in their horses in for the night or for several days. They had two liveries. Matt's livery checked out clean as a whistle, it was at Drew's Stable and Livery that they found two horses that had been ridden very hard. Drew was brushing them down and currying them, cussing the entire time that anyone would treat their horses this way. To his way of thinking, if they didn't take good care of their horses, they didn't deserve to have them!

"Drew, can you describe the two men who brought in the two horses?" Ren asked.

"Look for two assholes, and that will be them! They don't give two hoots for their horses or they never would have treated them like this!" Drew yelled and then seemed to settle down, "One's tall and one's short. They're both dirty and smelled. I sent them both up to the hotel to take a bath and get some decent food. I also made them pay me up front for the horses. They didn't even balk at the money up front. They both flipped me the coins and walked off with their saddle bags. You'll know them by their smell and the six guns in their holsters. They both had ivory handles." He paused and closed his eyes to better remember what they looked like. "The tall one had a scar on his hands, like from a fire or the scalding of hot water. I doubt it would slow him down in a gun fight, but it was there."

"Thank you, Drew. You've given us a lot to go on." Graham told him and Ren nodded. It sounded exactly who and what they were looking for. They headed toward the only hotel in town, the Graymont. It was the tallest building in town and boasted that they had over a dozen rooms to let. It also had a decent dining room and laundry. You could pull the cord and they would come and get your dirty clothes and bring them back a few hours later cleaner than you could believe.

They walked in the front door and looked over the register first. The clerk behind the counter didn't say a word. The last two entries were Keith Walker and Cody

Williams. Leah had told them that Buck's two friends were named Keith and Cody, they felt fairly confident that they had found the two men they were looking for. Graham asked for their room numbers and then saw several young men carrying buckets of water up the stairs to their rooms.

"Hell, Graham, lets let them get clean first. I don't want them stinking up our jail with their stink. We'll just sit down and wait for them to come down clean and smelling a lot better than they did before." Ren told Graham and they both sat down to wait. The register clerk was to give them a nod to make sure they got the right boys.

It took the better part of two hours for the two men to come down the stairs. It looked like they had had their clothes washed as well. The clerk gave them the nod, and Graham and Ren stood up their hands on their guns. "Howdy, boys. We're deputies of Trinity and we'd like to ask you to come down to the Sheriff's Office for a few questions..." Graham told them, but he didn't get to finish his sentence when both men went for their guns. Graham and Ren dived for cover and fired back at the two men on the stairs. Graham shot the short man and Ren got the taller scarred man in the arm but not before they shot Graham in the shoulder. He was still conscious as he watched Ren handcuff the two men. Then they sent for Doctor Harris and Sheriff Seth Wheeler. Thankfully, none of the other guests had been injured, just a few bullet holes to repair. Graham managed to stay conscious until the Sheriff got there and helped Ren take the two men back to the jail. Doctor Harris was going to get several men to help carry Graham back to his house to operate. When that was done, he'd come to the jail and see to the two men in jail. Even as they carried Graham back to his house, Doctor Harris asked someone to go tell Graham's wife what happened to her husband.

Leah was with Annalise sewing and talking away. They had become such good friends. When the gentleman came to the door, it was Leah who got up to see who it might be. She was a little leery answering the door to a stranger. He wasn't very tall, and he had a shock of gray hair sticking out from under his hat. He immediately pulled off his hat when he saw Leah. "Can I help you, Mr.?" Leah asked the little man.

"Yes'm you sure can, I'm looking for the Deputy's wife, he's been shot, and we just took him over to the Doc's house to get the bullet out. Doc told me to hurry on over here to let his wife know. Do you know the Deputy's wife?"

Leah's breath stopped in her throat. She turned white and looked like she was going to pass out. Annalise came lumbering up behind her, "Leah, what's wrong?"

"Graham's been shot! I'm sorry, Annalise, I've got to go to him!" By now, Leah was crying silently as she gathered up her purse. She turned to the little man, "Do you know Andy Renosso?" At his nod, she continued,

"Would you go get him and tell him that he needs to come home and stay with his wife?"

"I sure will little lady, do you know which house is Doc Harris's house?"

"No!" Leah started crying harder.

"Don't you worry none at all, I'll take you over there on my way to get Andy, how's that?" He took a good look at Annalise, "You ain't having that baby right, now are you?"

"No, I'm fine, just take care of Leah. I'll be fine when my husband gets here, he worries about me being all alone when I go into labor. I really don't think that today is the day! But thank you for asking and for going and getting my husband, Andy." Annalise waved them off and went to sit back down. She started praying for Graham to be all right.

Leah ran along the boardwalk to the Doc's house, Mr. Barton, the little gray-haired man, had a hard time keeping up with her. He opened up the front door of the doctor's house and yelled, "Here's his wife, Doc!" Leah went in eagerly to see Graham and how badly he was.

Doctor Harris took one look at Leah's white face and spoke sternly, "Don't you be fainting on me! I've got my hands full with your husband. Wash your hands and you can help me save his life!"

Leah did as she was asked. She would do whatever it took to make Graham well again. She did notice that he was unconscious and that the doctor had cut his shirt off his shoulder and chest. Blood seemed to be everywhere,

Graham's blood! "Tell me what you want me to do!" Leah told him in little more than a whisper.

"Good girl! Take my instruments out of the boiling water and place them on this tray, then start tearing five-inch strips of bandages off the sheets over on the counter. If I need something else, I'll yell for it. Right now, I need to concentrate on stopping the bleeding. "Doctor Harris went to work on Graham. Leah did exactly what the good doctor told her to do, but she prayed silently to herself over and over to God to keep Graham safe and to help the doctor make him well.

The surgery on Graham's shoulder took several hours. Once he found the bullet, he had to try and repair the damage that had been done to his shoulder. Leah kept him supplied with clean instruments and lots of bandages. Her eyes never left Graham's face. She loved him beyond all reason, she couldn't imagine her life without him. Sharing the little house had been heaven on earth, it's what she always imagined being married would be like. Laughing, talking, making decisions together, sharing their day...and their nights would be a wish come true. She didn't know how Graham felt about her. She knew he liked kissing her, he loved how they had made the little house into a comfy home. He loved her cooking and had even gained a couple of pounds from eating meals she had prepared. He was very complimentary about her sewing and washing of his clothes, he didn't mind helping her in the garden or in keeping the grass cut. She often saw a far away look in his eyes when he was watching her, his whole face softened and she thought it was yearning look, maybe for what he thought he couldn't have. Leah made several promises to herself that day, when not if Graham got better, they would have a real marriage if that's what he wanted. She only prayed that it was.

Leah helped Doctor Harris clean up his surgery and all the bloody sheets and bandages he had used. She re-sterilized all his instruments so he could use them on the two men Ren and Graham had captured. She also made a lot more bandages for him to use. Doctor Harris appreciated her quiet demeanor and her help. It would have taken him a lot longer by himself. He left her sitting beside Graham's bed holding his hand and talking softly to him. Harris knew that Graham would pull through, but he didn't think that Leah believed it yet. She would when he woke up. In the meantime, he had two other patients to remove the bullets. He packed up his medical bag, patted Leah's shoulder and left.

Graham was slowly regaining consciousness. He could have sworn he heard Leah's voice talking to him, but he figured he was either delirious or dreaming what he wished were happening. Leah...she was all he thought about these days. She made him so happy, and he hadn't even slept with her yet, but he sure wanted to! He didn't want her to think he was anything like Keifer Kutter trying to get her in bed, but he was having a hard time keeping his hands off of her! She was everything he had ever wanted in a wife, lover, and friend. As soon

182

as he woke up and knew he was going to live, he was going to talk to Leah and let her know how he felt. He loved her beyond all reason, she was quickly filling up his lonely heart and soul. The idea of her having his baby someday would be a dream come true. He wanted to be as good a father as his had been. He knew in his heart that both his parents would have loved Leah for her gentle ways and loving actions, and especially how good she was to him. He very much wanted to have a family, as long as Leah was part of it.

When Graham finally opened up his eyes, he was astonished to see Leah sitting by his bed holding his hand. Silent tears ran down her face and he could hear her whispering that he had to get better and come back to her. She didn't want to think about ever living without him. That's when Graham gave her hand a squeeze, when she turned to look at his face, Graham whispered, "I can't imagine living without you either, Leah. I...love...you, more than I can say. I've never told anyone I loved them before, I wish I had told my parents before they died, but I find it very easy to tell you how I feel."

"Oh, Graham! I love you too, so much! It's all I can think about! I just want you to get better and come back home to me. I...want...to be...a real wife to you, if you'll have me, that is..." Leah told him in return.

"Hell, yes I want you! There's nothing I'd like more than to be married to you for the rest of my life, but I didn't know how you felt, just how you make me feel...Lela Johnson, will you do me the honor of marrying me for real this time and for the rest of my life here on earth and making me the happiest man alive?"

Leah kissed him on both cheeks and on his lips, "Yes, I would marry you today, tomorrow and forever. Nothing could make me happier than to be your wife for real. I love you, Graham, making a home with you and having your babies is more than I ever thought would happen to me. You fill my heart and life with such joy!" Leah laughed, "Do we really have to go back to the preacher to marry us again?"

"No, the first time was legal, I just can't wait to make you really mine."

"Well, then, let's concentrate on getting you home again. I'll give you all the tender loving care that I can to get you better. And when you're healed, we'll have our marriage night, and I can love you in all the ways a woman loves her man. How does that sound?"

"Like heaven on earth! Now I just have to get better, did Doc tell you how long I have to stay in this bed?"

"For at least until he gets back from removing the bullets from the two men you and Ren arrested. He wanted to make sure that you weren't bleeding anymore. He said he'd arrange for someone to carry you home and put you into bed. Then it's up to me to spoil and pamper you to my heart's content. I do need to get word to Andy and Annalise that I won't be coming to work for the next couple of days while you're convalescing. I'll probably bring some sewing back to

184

the house with us. While you're sleeping and regaining your strength, I'll work on keeping the sewing caught up for Annalise. I might even have Andy bring her over to our house when he works, that way she won't be alone if she should go into labor. What do you think?" Leah asked, she was no longer crying, but her eyes still shone like two stars she was so happy.

"I think it's a good idea, that way Andy can get his work done without worrying about Annalise going into labor all alone. I'm married to a very thoughtful lady...a very beautiful lady...a very sexy lady. I'm the luckiest man alive, Leah, I love you..." Graham's voice dwindled away as he fell back asleep. Leah was feeling like she was sitting on a cloud, she was so happy. She was almost happy that Keifer had sent her to Trinity in the first place, otherwise she would have never met the man of her dreams!

It was late before Doctor Harris came back to his office and home. He walked into great smells coming from his kitchen, he followed his nose and found Leah in his kitchen taking out some fresh bread from the oven. Sitting on top of the oven was a thick beef stew. After so many hours bent over his patients, he had almost forgot how hungry he was.

"Sit down Doctor Harris. I thought you might be hungry by the time you finished with getting all those bullets out, I hoped you don't mind I made you up some stew, some bread, and there's a peach pie on the counter." She paused, "I wanted to say thank you for saving Graham for me. I don't know what I would do without him."

"Have you already eaten? If not, sit down, I usually have to eat alone. I never get to sit down for a meal with a beautiful young lady. It sure smells good in here!" Doctor Harris told her with a smile.

"There's warm water on the counter, wash up and I'll dish up. I haven't eaten either, so I would love to join you. I made some beef broth for Graham, he wasn't happy, but he drank it and fell back asleep. I hope that's all right?"

"I'm thrilled you got some liquids down him, with all the blood he lost that broth should hit the spot."

The two sat down and ate. They enjoyed each other's company. Harris found Leah to be funny, kind, and intelligent. Leah found Harris to be witty, smart, and caring. It was the beginning of a friendship that would last for many years.

CHAPTER 15

After they had eaten, Doctor Harris called on four strong men to carry Graham home on a litter, he sure didn't want him walking. He was worried that he would get dizzy from losing so much blood. Leah walked by his side and opened up the door to let the men in with Graham. They carefully lifted him onto the bed and left. Leah thanked them over and over again for helping her and her husband out.

Together, she and Graham got him out of his bloody clothes and into clean long johns. Graham was sweating from the exertion by the time they were done and fell asleep almost immediately. Leah gathered up all his clothes and put them in cold water to soak before she washed them. She hailed one of her neighbor's children to run down the street to the Renosso's to ask Andy to come and see them. It was dark when there was a knock on the door.

"Who is it?" Leah asked cautiously.

"Don't worry, Leah, it's me, Andy."

"Sorry, Andy, but after today I wanted to be safe rather than sorry! Thanks for coming so soon." Leah let Andy in and offered him a cup of coffee. He took her up on the offer.

"Thanks for sending Mr. Barton for me when you had to leave. I know it may sound silly, but I hate leaving her for any length of time for fear of her having the baby by herself." Andy paused and drank some of the coffee, "How's Graham doing?"

"Much better now that's he's home and the bullet's out! I don't mind telling you how scared I was that he wouldn't make it!"

"Graham's a tough guy, it'll take more than a few bullets to knock him down for good." They both laughed.

"Andy, I'm going to stay home for a few days to take care of Graham, I wondered if you would like to bring Annalise here during the days so we can sew and also so she won't be alone if she should go into labor. What do you think?" Leah asked him softly.

"Are you sure that you can handle Graham and my pregnant wife?" Andy asked. "That's a lot to ask of anyone. I sure don't want to leave her alone, but I have some jobs that need to be done, we need the money with the baby coming and all."

"No problem, Annalise and I can sit in the rockers and sew, and I'll make sure that she lays down every afternoon to get off those swollen legs and feet. If she should go into labor, I'll get one of the neighbor children to run and get the midwife and you. I'll help as much as I can. You and Annalise can even eat dinner here before you take her back home. That will be one less chore she will have to do each day until she delivers you a strong, healthy baby. I won't be able to weed your garden for a few days, but I'll make sure everything else is taken care of."

"You're a good friend, Leah. I will take you up on your offer to look after my wife. She'll like getting out of the house for a few days until you can come back to work for her. We'll both love having dinner with you each night. You let me know if you need anything from the Mercantile each morning, and I'll get it before I start working. How does that sound?" Andy smiled at Leah and the answer to his prayers.

"Perfect! I'll see you both tomorrow morning bright and early, and if you need me before then, just send someone down to let me know. If you could stop at the Mercantile and get us a large roast tomorrow, it should last us for several days. I'm pretty sure I have everything else we'll need." Leah walked him to the door.

"Thanks, Leah, we'll see you in the morning." Andy waved at Leah and hurried home. He breathed a sigh of relief for them coming up with a way to take care of Graham and Annalise.

Leah washed up the two coffee cups and then herself. She changed into her nightgown and lay down next to Graham as he slept. She didn't want to disturb him, but she did want to be as close to him as she possibly could. Within minutes she was asleep holding on to Graham's hand. Graham slept through it all, clearly exhausted from the surgery and the rest of his day.

Annalise and Andy came early with the roast and enough sewing to keep them busy for most of the day. Leah had already gotten up and transferred her clothes from the second bedroom to Graham's. She didn't want the Renosso's to know that they had been sleeping in separate bedrooms, or at least Annalise wouldn't know they had been sleeping apart. She knew that Andy knew all about the problems they had encountered and the solutions they had come up with. She also had biscuits and gravy waiting for all of them to eat. She thought that it was something that would go easy on Graham's stomach the day after surgery. She knew he would grumble and complain that he needed meat to get stronger, but Doctor Harris had warned her about feeding him heavy foods too soon.

Andy helped Graham go to the bathroom and then to help get him back into bed before he left to start work. He cautioned Annalise not to over do it today and to lay down and get plenty of rest. He'd see them at dinner time if not before. He kissed his wife and settled her into one of the rockers by the fireplace and walked out the door. Leah took a few minutes to make sure that Annalise had everything she needed before going in to help wash Graham and to help him eat his breakfast.

Graham wanted to get up, and Leah wouldn't let him. She was stubborn as a mule, but until Doctor Harris told him he could get up, he was staying in that bed, like it or not! Graham finally gave in and lay quietly as Leah shaved him and washed his face and hands before giving him some breakfast. Graham was starved! He dug into the biscuits and gravy like a man who hadn't eaten in days, but after only a few bites he slowed down and only managed to get down one biscuit. Leah had him drink some broth and a cup of coffee before he was sleeping again. She carried out the dishes and washrag to the kitchen to see how Annalise was doing. While she washed dishes, they chattered away.

Annalise was thrilled to be getting out of the house for a little while at least, it's not that she didn't like her home, she loved it. It had just been so long since she had been allowed to go anywhere, she was feeling a little claustrophobic!

She told Leah how nice her home was, it hadn't been that long ago that she had come to bring a house warming gift to Graham when he bought the house. It sure looked a lot different now! Leah was pleased that her new friend liked their home. Leah washed out Graham's bloody clothes and any other clothes they had that needed to be clean. After she hung them on the lines outside, she sat down beside her friend to sew. They were both extremely good seamstresses and their fingers fairly flew over the cloth and needles.

They stopped for lunch and Leah made Annalise lay down after lunch for at least an hour. Annalise didn't like it but her back hurt her so much she finally relented. While she slept, Leah took care of Graham. He was feeling better and drank an entire cup of broth and coffee and a half of sandwich. He told Leah he loved her several times and managed to steal several kisses before she made him take a nap as well.

She started the roast in the oven for dinner and peeled potatoes and carrots ready to be added later this afternoon. Doctor Harris came by to check out Graham and Deputy Ren came with him to give an update to Graham.

They were both pleased that Graham was doing so well.

"Glad to see you bounce back from the bullet, Graham. Both prisoners have had medical attention and are back to being their miserable selves. They've cussed us out, threatened us, and tried to bribe us! Sheriff Wheeler just laughed and told the boys to just keep digging their hole deeper and deeper! That's when they told us that they wired Keifer before they got shot, help was on the way, and we'd be sorry, real sorry by the time they got done with us. That's when we slammed the door to the jail and took off for the telegraph office. They not only telegraphed Keifer, they got a return telegram telling them he would arrive with reinforcements within two weeks. We didn't waste any time telegraphing the U.S. Marshalls Office that we needed reinforcements within two weeks. They promised us they would send as many as they could." Ren took a breath. "I took a ride out to the valley to tell Bo and all of them what was going on. Jo's back on the mend, but Molly is making her take it nice and slow until her headaches leave. Bo told us they would go into lockdown mode in a week and until Keifer and his men were caught, they'd continue to stay in that safe mode. Chief Enapay was sending even more of his men to the valley to help protect his friends. We just have to get you up and about and we'll be ready for them. How does that sound?" Ren asked.

"Sounds like you've got all the bases covered. You might want to warn all the saloons and businesses up and down Main Street about their eminent arrival. I don't want innocent citizens shot or killed when it comes to a showdown with Kiefer, and there will be a showdown. They won't go quietly no matter how out numbered they are. Doc how long before I can get back to doing my job?" Graham asked.

"I'd say you should be up and about in a week, it'll take longer to get full use of your arm though. But you should be able to go back to work by then. As long as you keep following your pretty nurse's instructions." Doctor Harris told them smiling. Leah ushered them out the door only to come back to Graham and cover his face with kisses.

"Graham I don't want you to go back to work too soon, I don't know what I would do if you got shot again so soon after the last time! I love you too much to let you go!" Leah told him quietly.

"Leah, I won't let that animal get anywhere close to you or to Charlie! And if I can help it, he won't get close to anyone to hurt again. He'll either be killed or arrested and sent to the Territorial Prison for the rest of his life for all the things he's done. Don't worry, I have too much to live for to not take every conceivable safety step I can. Don't you worry, I plan on living with you for the rest of our lives." Graham told her and kissed her again before she went out into the other room. That's when Leah heard Annalise. She was moaning and calling out to her!

Annalise had awoken from her nap to contractions that were coming one on top of the other. She didn't want her water to break and ruin the mattress on Leah's spare bedroom. Leah came in and immediately went into high gear getting the bed and Annalise ready to give birth. She took the oilcloth off the kitchen table and put it over the mattress and then covered it with all the newspapers she had collected for cutting into sheets to use in the outhouse. Then she placed a clean sheet over the bed. She helped Annalise out of her clothes and into one of her own clean nightgowns'. She washed her face and hands and told her to hold on, she was going for help.

She knocked or rather pounded on her neighbor's door until they answered. She sent someone to go get Hilde Schultz, the midwife, and for Andy Renosso. Then she hurried back to her own house to get water boiling and to get things ready to usher in a new life into the world. Leah had never helped with giving birth to a baby before, but she had sure helped with plenty of births of animals out at her parents' farm growing up.

She hoped it wouldn't be too much different than that. She found the time to tell Graham what was happening. He told her he was fine, just concentrate on helping Annalise get through labor all right.

Andy was the first to arrive, he must have run all the way because he was out of breath when he walked through the door. Leah asked him to go back to his house and get some diapers and clothes to put the baby in when it arrived, they'd use a box for a cradle until they could get Annalise and the baby home after they were done. Andy kissed Annalise and told her not to deliver that baby until he got back and ran back out the door.

Hilde Schultz was the next to arrive, she approved of all Leah had done and checked Annalise over to see how far along she was. It was while she was checking Annalise that her water broke. Hilde, as she insisted on being called, said that would move things a little bit faster. She assured the expectant mother everything was just fine, they just had to wait a little longer and she would be holding her baby for the very first time. Then she turned to Leah.

"If you can find some bricks to put in the fireplace to heat, it would be very helpful. Once the baby is born, I'll clear out the mucus from its mouth and cut the cord. It'll be up to you to give the baby its first bath and get it dressed. It needs to be done fairly quickly, so it doesn't get chilled. That's what the bricks are for, we'll put them all around the box you've got ready for the baby.

I'm going to use that boiling water to sterilize my scissors and string, I'll be right back." Hilde was one of the most self-assured women Leah had ever met. She also oozed confidence. Leah sure felt a lot better having her here than trying to deliver that baby by herself!

Andy arrived shortly after Hilde had examined Annalise, she approved of all the baby clothes he had brought with him. Hilde told Leah to go ahead and throw the vegetables she had peeled in with the roast. She'd be too busy in a few minutes to do anything else but take care of the newborn baby. Leah didn't need to be told twice. She was doing exactly what Hilde told her to do!

It didn't seem very long at all before Hilde was telling Annalise to push. She stationed Andy at her back and had him help in supporting her as she pushed. Her face was red, and she was perspiring heavily. Leah washed off her face and her hands to help make her feel more comfortable, but Leah didn't think that Annalise was even aware that she was there. All her efforts were concentrated on getting that baby out healthy, and as quickly as possible!

Within minutes, Hilde cried out, "I see the head, just a little bit more Annalise. Just give me time to clear out the mucus from its little mouth. That's it, girl, push that baby out!" No sooner had she said the words, that a small baby came forth. Quickly Hilde cut the cord and handed the baby over to Leah. It was still and not crying. Leah looked at Hilde, "What do I do?"

"Swing it by its heels and give a gentle swat to its bottom, it usually does the trick!" Hilde told her as she worked over Annalise.

Leah did just that, she gently swung the baby by its heels and swatted the little bottom. The baby let forth with a cry that continued to get louder as it protested its ill treatment. No one had even noticed what sex the child was, boy or girl! "It's a little girl, Annalise, she's beautiful just like her mother! There, there little one, just let me get you cleaned up and I'll introduce you to your mother and father!" Leah crooned to the tiny baby. Leah thought trying to give the baby its first bath was like trying to bathe a greased piglet, she was soon as wet as the baby was!

By the time Leah had the baby clean and diapered and dressed, she had stopped crying but her tiny fist was in her mouth as she tried to suckle. Hilde had Annalise all cleaned up and ready to hold her baby. Tears ran down both Andy's and Annalise's faces, they were so proud of their baby and glad that everything had gone so well. Hilde just stood back to admire her handiwork. Bringing new life into the world was the most satisfying job she could imagine doing. She cleared her throat interrupting the new parents counting toes and fingers and admiring their work, "What you going to name that baby?"

Andy smiled and kissed Annalise's head, "We want to name the baby Annaleigh. It's after Annalise and Leah, without which my Annalise would have been all alone today when the baby came. We owe much to her friend." Leah was touched and felt so honored, she nodded at both Annalise and Andy and little Annaleigh and hurried to tell Graham what a wonderful gift she had just been given!

Annalise, Annaleigh, and Andy stayed for a week. Then she was taken back to her own house. It was good to have so many guests in their home because it gave Graham something to do besides argue that he had to get back to work! Andy was a blessing, he went in and talked to Graham every day and told him all that was being done to prepare for Kutter and his band of cutthroats to arrive. Andy told Graham that they still had more than a week before he was expected to arrive. He was to heal first so that he would be an asset to the town instead of a one-handed liability. Graham heard him but he didn't like what he heard. He was getting out of bed every day, but needed help getting dressed. He wasn't sleeping as much, he just wasn't used to being so idle all day long.

Leah took the time to take him outside with her to watch her weed the garden. He was soon on his knees helping her. They did a lot of talking, laughing, and kissing. Neither Graham nor Leah were patient about their inability to make love yet. Leah did everything in her power to make things easier on Graham. She even took him over to the Renosso's to pick the weeds out of their garden one day. Graham smiled all day just to get out of the house for a while and feel like he was useful again!

Leah loved having Annalise and the baby at her house. She spent long hours talking to Annalise and watching her take care of Annaleigh. She was so soft and cuddly, she even had Graham hold her with one hand and arm. They both had the same thought, someday this would be their baby in their arms.

Annalise, Annaleigh, and Andy went back to their own home in a week. The same amount of time Doctor Harris made Graham stay in bed or at least at home. He couldn't wait to get back to work and find out if the men he shot were wanted by the law and had wanted posters out on them. He also couldn't wait for the Renosso's to leave and go home, so that he could make love to his wife. He couldn't believe that she loved him, too, and making her his wife was on his mind constantly.

Leah was so busy taking care of him, the Renosso's, taking care of her own garden and Annalise's, and keeping up with all the sewing that needed to be done to keep her business going kept Leah running from early morning to late at night. She loved sleeping in Graham's arms every night and knew that he was only counting the days until he could love her as he wished. Leah wanted that too, but she had not had a very good experience with Keifer Kutter. She worried that she might somehow disappoint Graham, and that was the last thing she wanted to do. She decided that the best thing to do would be to talk with him about her worries.

It wasn't easy finding time when it was just the two of them in their tiny little house. She resolved to talk to Graham tonight before she fell asleep!

She helped Andy get Annalise and the baby home and set up with dinner on the stove. She told Annalise that she would be over first thing in the morning to wash diapers and clothes for her, to weed her garden and to finish the sewing orders they had waiting.

"Leah, you've been so good to us, why don't you come in a little later tomorrow morning. That will give you time to set your house in order after having three extra house guests all week! I can't tell you how much we loved the time we spent with you and Graham, but it is good to get back to our own little home and start being a mother to Annaleigh and back to being a wife to Andy." Annalise told her over and over again, "Thank you for everything! I promise to do the same for you and Graham when you have your first child!"

Leah hugged her and gave a kiss to little Annaleigh, waved good-bye to Andy and hurried home to Graham.

Graham wasn't at home when she got there. He left a note telling her he was at the Sheriff's Office and he would be home in a few hours. He signed it 'Love, Graham.' Leah wasted no time in stripping the bed in the spare bedroom and washing all the sheets. Then she took her wash water and scrubbed all the floors. She started making loaves of bread and planned what they would have for dinner. Sometime before dinner, she wanted to take a bath and wash her hair. She wanted everything to be perfect for her and Graham tonight, and she prayed over and over again that she wouldn't be a disappointment for him when they made love for the first time.

CHAPTER 16

Graham enjoyed being back at work again. He was also looking forward to being alone with Leah for the first time since they had both proclaimed their love for each other. Tonight, he was going to be able to love Leah all night long! There was a spring in his step and a smile on his face. He stopped in to see Jonah and Lottie and to see how they were doing on one of his many boardwalk checks throughout the day. He knew Leah would want to know how her good friend was doing.

The store was jumping. The people of Trinity really liked how the store had been changed and loved coming in and using the little baskets to pick up their needs. Lottie was charming and very helpful, and Jonah was Jonah. He wasn't smiling, but he was taking care of customers right and left. At least he wasn't growling at anyone, Graham thought!

He finally asked if Jonah could join him in the supply room for a few minutes. He saw Jonah look for Lottie and give her a nod. Lottie responded with a smile and then she went back to speaking to the customer she was currently helping.

Jonah followed Graham to the supply room. His first words out of his mouth, "It's good to see you up and about, Graham. You had us all worried! What's up?"

"Not much, I just wanted to see how you and Lottie were doing and to let you know that we expect Keifer and his men by the end of the week." Graham told him. "Have you and Lottie planned on what you're going to do if one of his men or Keifer walks into the store?"

Jonah gave a big sigh; his face was troubled as he answered. "I'd like to say if I see any of the sons of bitches, I'll just shoot to kill, but I know I can't with Lottie and other customers in the store who could get hurt in the process. I've told Lottie at the first sign of trouble, she's to head upstairs to her rooms and stay there until I tell her to come down. But you know Lottie, she has to argue about every decision I make around here. She's determined to help get the world rid of Keifer and his men with us. She wants to hold a gun and get on the roof and help us out. I don't want to let her do that. I'm having a rough time imagining her getting shot or killed! I...couldn't live with myself if I let anything happen to her after all we've done to keep her safe." He paused and ran his hand over his face. "But you know Lottie, nobody is going to tell her what to do. I just might have to carry her upstairs kicking and screaming and tie her down to stay out of trouble! Any suggestions?"

"I like the last option of carrying her upstairs and tying her down." Graham told him with a smile.

"Although I don't know if you'll have that much advance time when they arrive. They might come in all at once, or only a few at a time. Then again, they might split their forces and send half to the town and half out to the valley. We just know that trouble is coming, and we have to be prepared for one way or another. If you do happen to see any of them, try to get word to us at the Sheriff's office, we'll be here to back you up, provided that we aren't already involved with the rest of his crew somewhere else in town. Just be alert and ready." Graham and Jonah shook hands and Graham left while Jonah went back to the counter to help the next customer. Time was running out.

Graham stopped on his way home to talk to Andy and to check on Annalise and Annaleigh. The little family was doing very well, mother and daughter were sleeping, and Andy looked like he needed a nap as well! Graham picked a few flowers before he came to his own little home. He found his breath was coming in short gasps as he anticipated the evening with Leah. He opened the front door to delicious smells coming from the stove and to clean spotless floors. Leah had opened up the windows and fresh air blew gently through the little house. His Leah was standing at the stove and gave Graham a tremulous smile. Graham could tell she was as nervous as he was, maybe even more!

Graham walked over to his wife and kissed her, really kissed her. Several seconds later he drew away and gave the flowers to Leah. "Now that's how I want to be greeted in the future! Something smells good, and you look good enough to eat yourself! The house smells and looks clean and back to normal. Somebody's been very busy!"

Leah smiled and told him, "I wanted tonight to be special, kind of like our wedding night...So I made your favorite dinner. Sit down and I'll put it on the table. I know you must be starving. How does your arm feel? You didn't overdo it, today did you?"

"It's a little tender, but it felt good enough to get back to work again. I stopped by and talked to Jonah and Andy. Everybody is doing fine. Jonah looked a little haggard, I think that Lottie is giving him trouble again over what he tells her to do. She is not going along with everything quietly. When Keifer and his men come to town, she told Jonah that she wanted to take a rifle and get on the roof. She wants to help us get rid of the entire gang. Can you believe that?"

"You know that's not a bad idea, Graham." Leah told a very surprised Graham. "Charlie's dad had all the girls know how to shoot and get game. I'd say that Charlie is an excellent shot, and if she's mad enough, she could shoot down every one of those men without batting an eye! She might even be a help with Keifer. He's not going to come in and announce that he's here, he'll probably have a couple of his men on some of the roofs shooting down at you! Maybe I should start carrying a gun, too!"

"Now hold on, I know you have that old Colt you took from Keifer, but I want you safely out of the way when bullets start flying! I don't know what I'd do if you were to get hurt in the shoot out with Kutter's men! I want you and Annalise and her baby to be safe and sound out of sight from all the gun play." Graham paused. "If you'll feel safer carrying the gun with you, just in case...all right. But under no circumstances do I want you out of the house, either ours or the Renosso's. Do we agree on that?"

"I promise not to do anything stupid, like tracking them down and trying to be a heroine, but if one of those low life's come to my door, I'll send them to kingdom come!" Leah told him with spirit.

They spent the rest of the evening in quiet talk of what was happening in the rest of the town. They both took a bath and retired early to the solitude of their bedroom. Leah stood before Graham in her white nightgown with her hair flowing down her back. Graham thought she was the most beautiful woman he'd ever seen. He was dressed in only his pants from his bath. He crossed the few remaining steps to touch Leah and kiss her gently on the lips. "You are so beautiful, Leah, my Leah!"

Leah smiled at him tenderly, but with a solitary tear in her eye. "I love you Graham, more than I ever thought I could love any man. I'm...sorry that I'm not the virginal bride you deserve...I don't want you to be disappointed tonight as we make love for the first time."

"Stop right there, Leah. Let's get one thing understood right now! If Keifer hadn't treated you the way he did, you would never have left Paducah and come to Trinity. I never would have met the love of my life. Because of Keifer, I met you and was lucky enough to get married to you before you realized there might have been other options open to you. I hate the man for all he's done in his life, but most of all I hate him for making you so unhappy. But I will also thank him with my last breath for sending you to Trinity...I love you, Leah, you could never disappoint me. Not in anything you do, but especially not when we make love. We will be making love to each other, not just me making love to you. I want it to be perfect for both of us, and to do that, we need to put Keifer out of our minds and come to each other as one. Can you do that Leah?" Graham asked her quietly. He knew that if he didn't get to hold and kiss his Leah in the next few seconds, he'd never be able to stop.

Tears ran down Leah's face and she threw herself into Graham's arms covering his face in kisses and telling him over and over again how very much she loved him. Needless to say, nature took over. It took little time at all to remove Leah's nightgown and Graham's pants. They were both a little in awe of each other's bodies. Leah thought Graham looked like the Greek statues she had seen in a book while she was in school. He was finely chiseled and muscled everywhere she looked. Graham couldn't believe how perfect Leah was. She had luscious breasts and a tiny waist, the perfect derriere and long slender legs, he could just imagine them wrapped around him. She simply took his breath away. They fell into bed kissing and touching all the places they had only dreamed of being able to caress. It took little time at all for Graham to raise himself above Leah and thrust into her making her his for all time. Leah couldn't get over how good everything felt. She couldn't get her breath as she was meeting Graham thrust for thrust. Both reached their climax at the same time. Neither could get their breath back quickly. Graham reveled in how glorious their love making was, never had it felt this good, never had he lost his control so quickly. He couldn't seem to hold himself back. Leah was in much the same state as Graham, she couldn't believe how making love could feel so wonderful and absolute. They turned to each other again and this time made love again and again all throughout the night. It was the perfect wedding night for both of them.

Lottie wanted to know what Graham had told Jonah in the storeroom. There wasn't time during the day to get any time alone with him to ask. Ever since that kiss in the storeroom when they were organizing and cleaning it, Jonah seemed to be avoiding being alone with her. Tonight, Lottie was going to change that. She wanted answers and she was determined to get them.

Jonah had sent her upstairs to get their dinner ready, he was shutting down the Mercantile for the night. Lottie had put in a roast in the early afternoon and had ran upstairs to add potatoes and carrots later on, all she had to do was serve it and make gravy. Lottie felt good that Jonah liked her cooking. He may not like her too much, but he sure did enjoy her meals over the ones he had been living on from the café across the street. Even her bread, rolls, and biscuits were lighter and tasted so good warm from the oven with butter melting even as they ate it. Jonah came up the stairs and sat down in one of their two chairs. He loved the way Lottie had made the spare rooms into a home. It was warm and inviting. She had even found the time to recover that old couch that was in the parlor. She had covered it with a muted plaid canvas in browns and tans and made pillows of brown and tan to sit on it as well. She had also found an old dark brown rug over at the resale store and it lay in front of the rocker and couch. The spare bedroom had been cleaned out and ready for guests to stay if they wanted them. It was heaven on earth to come upstairs to a wonderful meal with Lottie. She was getting through to him. He couldn't get her out of his mind. Not during the day, and the nights were pure hell. If only he hadn't kissed her...then he wouldn't have known how perfect, she was in his arms. He didn't want to think how lonely he was going to be after she left. And more than that, he didn't want to think of her being in someone else's arms and life.

"What did Graham want to talk to you about this afternoon?" Leah got right to the point.

"He came by to let us know to expect Keifer and his men in a few days, probably by the end of the week. He wanted to know if we had a plan to get you to safety if we should see any of his men come into the store...I told him what I wanted to happen, and then I told him what you wanted to happen. I don't want anything to happen to you Lottie...I couldn't live with myself if it did." Jonah told her and even reached across the table to grab her hand.

"I do understand, Jonah, but I don't want anything to happen to you either. I couldn't live with myself if it did...You've given up your home, your solitary lifestyle for me and to keep me safe. I'm sorry for fighting you every step of the way, but I'm not used to taking orders or for anyone else to tell me what to do. I haven't made things easy for you, and I'm sorry. But my pa taught all his girls how to shoot, and shoot well, I might add. If I can help defeat Keifer and his men and keep you safe, I'm going to do it regardless what you or Graham says." And then Leah got up and crossed to where Jonah was sitting and kissed him full on the mouth.

At the first touch of Leah's kiss, Jonah grabbed hold of Leah and pulled her down to his lap and returned her kisses over and over again. He couldn't help himself. "Charlie...we should stop while I still can...I want you too much to tempt fate."

Charlie was thrilled that Jonah wanted her, she certainly wanted him! Slowly Jonah pulled Charlie's arms from around his neck, kissed her once more and directed her back to her own chair. "Kissing you could become a habit, Charlie." He said softly. But Charlie heard and smiled. They finished their meal in silence. Jonah stood up to leave and then turned around and kissed Charlie again. "Good night..." He whispered.

Charlie sighed and spent the rest of the night cleaning up the dishes and reliving the evening with Jonah. She realized how very much she loved the man and hoped that he was beginning to love her as well.

Keifer Kutter was indeed on his way. He and a dozen of his men were riding with him. They were taking the train, because it was the fastest and easiest way to travel. They had an entire railcar to themselves and another boxcar for their horses. The men had to take turns staying with the horses making sure they had food and water and constantly shoveling out the manure that thirteen horses can produce! But Kutter promised them some fun at the end of the trail, they were going to be able to shoot up the town and raise all kinds of Holy Hell to get what they wanted.

Walker and Williams had sent a telegram that they had seen the little white-haired girl and the mother near a town called Trinity. They had yet to see Charlie or Lela, but they were sure the Bellamy's were all there. That was enough for Keifer. If they couldn't find Lela, they would take the red-haired Bellamy girl. Either way he'd go back with two good looking girls to add to his family of whores. One woman was almost as good as another to his way of thinking, and women were only good for two reasons. The first was to ease a man's needs, the second was to cook. He enjoyed good food and he couldn't abide not being well fed. He even had brought along a chef to cook his meals on the train. With a little cash, his chef was let into the kitchen of the dining car and his meals were seen to. Now as soon as he caught Charlie and Lela or her sister Dani, all his needs would be seen to!

Keifer was not used to being thwarted by anyone. He wasn't that big of a man, but he was mean clear through. Men much larger than he was were scared of him and what kind of reactions he might have in any situation. He had been known to kill a man over the minor slight of just bumping into him. He paid his men well for their 'skills' and to their loyalty. He didn't care what kind of men they were, he wanted action and he wanted it now. His men knew that, and they jumped to do his bidding. They all knew that he was being inconvenienced by having to go after the Bellamy bitch and they hoped Lela, too. They didn't want to see what Keifer would do if he only found one of the girls.

During the War Between the States, Keifer was every bit as lethal and dangerous as the James brothers or the Younger boys. He enjoyed killing and raiding, when the war ended and they became wanted men for what they did in the war, the James boys and the Younger's turned to robbing to get what they wanted. Keifer liked to think he was smarter than that. He became a 'respected' business man in a town that was expected to grow. Many of the stores were just barely holding on, Keifer came in with money he had gained from the war and became their partners. Between legal and illegal means, he was able to obtain almost complete control of the town of Paducah in a year or two. Money rolled in especially when Keifer came up with such beautiful, young girls to service his men and half the population of Paducah. He used whatever means was called for. He drugged some of them, used physical force on a few of them, and kept them all on a very short leash. They all knew what would happen if they upset him or disappointed him. It had all worked like a charm until Lela Johnson. She didn't care about the drugs, the alcohol, or the physical abuse. She wasn't going to become one of his upstairs girls no matter what, she would rather be dead than become a whore. Lela just might get her wish when Keifer got hold of her again. He had a lot of anger resting inside of him. Not only did he want to see her as one of his whores, he wanted to see her suffer because of her disobedience. He couldn't take the chance that another of his women would run just like she did.

He'd be damned if he'd chase his women all over the territory to get them back. Women were easy to get, beautiful women were a little harder to get and keep, as Keifer had found out with Lela and Charlie. But all that was going to change when he got his hands on both of them. After he was finished with them, he'd turn them over to his men, who were neither gentle nor patient. By the time they got back to Paducah, they'd be begging him to let them work for him in whatever capacity that was. God help them if they thwarted him again!

Jo was healing slowly from her concussion. She kept getting headaches and feeling dizzy for several days and even weeks after her attack. She was grateful for Molly's care and that of her mother, she was even more grateful for Wolf's quick action that removed her from the stranger's agenda. She stopped wandering the woods alone. She would wait for Wolf, and together they would roam the hills and forests. Wolf loved this time with her, he vowed he'd never let anyone hurt her ever again. Chief Enapay was not happy that three strangers had invaded the very forests they were sent to keep safe, he sent more men and instructed them to patrol and keep watch so that anyone coming or leaving the valley were watched and their movements were immediately reported to Bo or Boone. He had promised his protection and he was determined to make sure that they had it. After all, he was a man of his word.

Miriam's due date was fast approaching. Even with caring for the cabin, the garden, Mason and Tate, she found time to make everything she felt she would need for the baby. Miriam hadn't looked forward to Mason at the end of her first pregnancy. By the time she was pregnant with him, she knew what kind of man she had married. He answered any kind of response with his fists and his brute strength. He was lazy but made sure that Miriam did her work and some of his too. As a result, Mason had come early. He had been so small, Miriam didn't know if he would survive or not. Part of her wanted him too, and another knew that he would be better off without having to live in his Pa's world. She did her best to make sure that if her late husband was angry, he took it out on her and not her son. But Mason saw enough to make him steer clear of him as much as possible. Mason was such a good boy, he had blossomed under Tate's care. He praised him and his efforts and was so patient teaching him how to plant, plow, hunt, or even chop wood. Tate was just as patient and loving with her, she didn't know that men like him existed. She loved him and hoped to give him many more sons and even a few daughters. Tate had told her he didn't care if the baby was a boy or girl, he just wanted both Miriam and the baby to be healthy and safe when all was said and done. She had known that her baby was due in the late summer, but it seemed that it had a mind of its own. The baby dropped and even walking was harder for Miriam to do. Getting up off the ground after she had weeded her garden was almost impossible to do.

Because of the threat of Keifer Kutter, Tate was staying closer to home than usual. Nobody needed any cabins built, thank heavens, but they did need to put in a cellar and a smoke house for the Bellamy's before they started threshing or cutting crops. He sure felt bad abut Ed dying and leaving his wife and three daughters. But he would go to Hell and back for him and his family, Ed had saved his life several times during the war and he owed him for letting him get a second chance at happiness. Miriam and Mason were his world, he loved how special she made him feel, and Mason was everything he had ever wanted in a son. He didn't think of his real pa, he was a gutless man who preyed on the weak with his fists. He drank too much and then took out his temper on Miriam. Nothing like that would ever happen to her again, Tate made a promise to her and to Mason, that he would protect them no matter what. He intended to do just that, regardless of Keifer and his band of cut throats. He didn't know Keifer, but he had seen the aftermath of he and his men in Quantrill's Raiders. Too many innocent people had died and suffered because of him and his kind. The war was over, and it was time that Keifer was made to atone for his sins.

Molly was keeping close tabs on Miriam and Violet both. With as much work as they both did, it wasn't without certain risks to the length of their pregnancies. As much as her baby had dropped and turned, Molly looked for her to be the first to deliver and probably pretty soon at that. She made sure that they had an oilcloth and a pile of newspapers ready for her delivery, and she kept her medicine bag packed and ready at all times. She was glad that their treks into the forest for berries and such had been curtailed for a short time until Keifer Kutter and his men were caught, even the few weeks they waited could mean the difference of Miriam and Violet delivering a baby big enough to survive here in the Montana Territory. She knew that she would do everything she could do to keep them safe.

Molly's own twin boys were growing by leaps and bounds. They were old enough now to try and crawl or scoot off the blanket she placed them on. She had to keep a close eye on them to keep them safe, she knew that eating dirt wouldn't hurt them too much, but she also didn't want it to happen on her watch! Bo, Boone, and Jo were so helpful in keeping them safe whenever she had to go check on Miriam or Violet or any of the others.

It was late June when Tate sent Mason to go get Molly, Miriam was in labor. Molly left the twins with Boone and Jo, and Bo took her over to the Adams cabin. After an examination, Molly declared that Miriam was indeed in labor. Her contractions were strong and fairly close together. She didn't expect a very long labor. She readied the bed and washed down Miriam, all the while talking very soothing and calmly to Miriam. She was upset. She knew that it was too soon for the baby to come, it would be too small. She didn't want to lose Tate's baby, she wanted it with every fiber of her being.

Molly told her that it was summer. The cabin was warm, and they kept it warm during the much cooler nights. They would put warm bricks in the cradle to help keep the baby's temperature warm enough that it wouldn't get chilled. She assured Miriam that they would do everything they could do to deliver this baby safe and sound into her loving arms. "Have faith, Miriam. You have gone through so much to get where you are today. You have a loving husband and son, you are safe in a beautiful valley, and are surrounded by a wealth of friends. Put your trust in God, he won't let you down." Molly told her when her water broke, and she was cleaning up the mess and helping change Miriam into a dry gown.

Mason was a huge help, boiling water, showing her where they kept the oilcloth and extra newspapers, getting a basin of warm water to wash the baby in, and even of rounding up some little clothes for the baby to be dressed in when it was cleaned up and washed. Tate had kept the fireplace and the cook stove filled and ready for just about anything. He also placed several bricks in the fireplace and tore several towels into pieces to wrap them in for the cradle. He was sweating bullets watching Miriam bring their baby into this world, he heard her concerns to Molly about the baby coming early and not being big enough to survive. He'd take the pain instead of Miriam if he could, and he was determined that if they had a baby that survived its birth, he would do everything he could do to make sure that it lived to adulthood. He'd waited so long to find a wife, he didn't want to lose her now.

It was late in the day, when strangers were spotted on the edge of their property in the valley. Bo told Tate to stay with Miriam but to stay armed and ready. He brought Jo, Boone, and the twins over to Tate's cabin, so he could watch over them as well. Every able-bodied man was going to make sure they never reached any closer to their homes.

Molly suddenly wished that she had a dozen hands and arms. Miriam pushed out a baby within minutes of hearing that men were coming to their valley. Molly cleared the mucus out of the baby's mouth and cut the cord. The baby was still and turning blue. Molly took the baby by its heels and swung the baby, gently tapping the baby on its tiny bottom. The baby seemed to take a huge breath and started crying, a weak mewling at first and then as it cried it got much stronger and louder. Molly was thrilled, the baby was small, but not too small. It would survive, she hadn't yet looked to see whether the baby was a boy or a girl. She handed the baby off to Tate to give it its first bath and to quickly get the baby dressed.

"Congratulations, Tate, Miriam, you have a baby girl! She's small, but not too small and she sounds like she's got a good set of lungs. You keep her warm and fed and she'll be just fine. Now let's get you cleaned up Miriam and then you can hold her." Molly had to wipe the tears from her own eyes before she started on Miriam. Miriam was crying and so was Tate, he was afraid he'd drop the tiny little girl, but he was smiling and grinning from ear to ear!

"God, she's beautiful, Miriam! She looks just like you! Dark hair and dark eyes, she even has a dimple in her cheek like Mason! She's slippery as a greased pig, but I'll take good care of her. That's it little one, Papa's got you now, and nothing and nobody will ever hurt you again..." Tate continued to talk softly to the crying baby while he gently washed her and put her in a dry diaper and warm gown and booties and then he wrapped her in several blankets to keep her body heat contained.

Molly finished with Miriam and watched as Tate gently put the baby into her waiting arms. Then he kissed her and thanked her for giving him such a wonderful gift. Together they counted her fingers and toes and marveled how beautiful she was.

"Any ideas on what you're going to name the newest Adams addition?" Molly asked as she wadded up the dirty sheets and soiled newspapers.

Miriam smiled a very tired but contented smile, "You told me to have faith, Molly, what do you think about calling her Faith, Tate?" She waited for his response.

"Faith Miriam Adams sounds just perfect to me, love." Tate told her with a kiss. Molly left the happy couple to soak the sheets and dispose of the newspapers.

She found Jo feeding one of the twins and Boone feeding the other one. She immediately started making something to eat for all of them. She heaved a big sigh of relief that everything had turned out so well. When Mason came in with another load of firewood, she smiled and told him, "Mason you have a little sister. They've decided to call her Faith. Why don't you go in and see her for yourself? Your family has been very blessed, they have a son and a daughter. Congratulations!"

Boone and Jo told him congratulations as well, and everyone was smiling. Molly's hands made dinner, but her mind was on her husband and every other able-bodied man in the valley. She didn't want any trouble coming to their homes, but she would be prepared. She placed Boone's gun near his chair, placed her own derringer in her pocket, and made sure that the rifle was loaded and within reaching distance. She kept one eye on their dinner, and one eye out the window watching for whatever came their way.

CHAPTER 17

Keifer Kutter had split his forces into two groups. Half of his men would go to the valley and look for Charlie and Lela. He didn't figure a bunch of farmers would stand a chance against his ruthless men who would stop at nothing to get the job done at any costs. The other half of his crew would follow him into town. He had no qualms about holding the town hostage to get what he wanted. He didn't think that they would have the guts to stand up against his men or himself. If need be, he would burn down the town to get to the women and to achieve his goals. Those women had made him go to the ends of the earth to find them and find them he would no matter what it took to get it done. They would wish they were dead before he was done with them!

Keifer made several mistakes in his thinking. The biggest one was that they didn't know he and his army of thugs were coming and the second was that he was just dealing with a bunch of farmers.

The valley was filled with men who had fought in the War Between the States together and they worked together to form a plan of attack. They had the added bonus of Chief Enapay and all his braves. The Chief was a great strategist in his own thoughts of warfare and battle. He and Bo made an almost unstoppable duo. Their plan was to present a solid front line, but also to surround the men on all sides with the Sioux warriors. They would command the interlopers to throw down their weapons and capture them, if they did not concede, then they would fight. Since they had the edge on the number of men involved, they felt they would have the winning hand.

Keifer's men did indeed ride into the valley. They saw the line of defense set up by the 'farmers' and almost laughed at how easy they thought their victory would be. Then the Indians showed themselves, suddenly it didn't look as easy.

"Throw down your weapons and that means the ones in your boots as well and the extra guns you have positioned behind your backs. You have until the count of five to comply. If you don't, we will open fire on you and your men." Bo shouted when he felt they had come forward close enough. Every gun, every bow and arrow was pointed at Keifer's six men. They glanced at each other and at the odds of their coming out alive. When Bo came to the number four, Keifer's men opened fire on them!

Bo's friends and the Sioux warriors returned the fire! It was shot after shot being fired, Bo's men had taken refuge behind several trees and large stones, so they weren't sitting ducks. The Sioux warriors never stayed still long enough to get hit. It took little time at all to rid the world of six more thugs. Bo's side had received three injuries. Bo sent Red and the two Indians who were injured over to Tate's home where Molly could give them the care they needed to mend. He and the others loaded the six bodies into a wagon to take into town. He had Sam Greer and Calvin Jackson to each take one of the raider's horses, he gave the other four to Chief Enapay and his men. They divided up the guns and knives among the settlers and the Indians.

"Chief Enapay we wish to thank you for your help in keeping our valley safe. You and your people are always welcome here. We will share our meat and cattle with you and the rest of our bounty. If you are ever in need, send word and we will come running to always stand beside our friends. We're going to take the bodies into town. I'm not sure what we'll find when we get there. Would you and your men stand guard until we get back? I don't like leaving without knowing what still might be out there waiting for us." Bo asked.

"We will stay and guard each house and farm. We are honored to have you and your friends as our brothers." Chief Enapay nodded and gave the signal to disperse and go back to guarding the valley. One of his men led the four horses away to disappear in the woods.

Bo and the rest proceeded to split up and tell their wives that they were safe, all was well, and that they were going into town with the bodies and to help get rid of the rest of Keifer Kutter's man. Bo didn't for a minute think that the six men were all the threat that Keifer brought with him. He wasn't going to stop until Keifer, and his men were no longer a threat to anyone else in the valley.

Molly had tears in her eyes when Red and the two Indians appeared at Tate's cabin. She didn't bat an eye before she was washing and disinfecting the wounds and making sure they were all right. Bo walked in while she was caring for one of the Indians and she took a minute to throw herself into his arms to kiss and hug him knowing that he wasn't wounded.

"Tate, we're taking the bodies to town. Chief Enapay and his men are going to stay and watch over the valley until we get back to determine if all the threat is gone." Bo told his old commander and wagon master. Then Bo grinned and asked, "What did Miriam have? Are you a father yet?"

"She did, "Tate grinned and slapped him on the back, "I am now the proud father of a son in Mason, and a daughter with little Faith. I'd say our little family is complete. Do you need me to stay here or to go with you and the others?"

"I'd feel better if you'd stay here to take care of any problems that might arise. We'll take the rest of the bodies and the rest of our men to go into town to help out Graham and Jonah. These men were not going to quit without a fight, and I don't think that Keifer will be any different. We had the extra men with the Sioux, they might need some extra guns with us to sway the battle to our side. Either way the bodies have to get to town, and I'll feel a whole better with extra guns going with us." Bo explained. "By the way, we had six horses left over, I made sure that Sam and Calvin each took a horse and gave the other four to Chief Enapay for their help in the fight. We also split up all the guns and knives the six men had on them. I swear it was like an arsenal they carried with them, the only thing they were missing was a Gatling gun and a cannon!"

"It sounds like a good exchange to me, good luck on the trip to town. I'll make sure that everything stays good here in the valley." Tate and Bo shook hands and Bo kissed Molly before he took off. Molly wiped a tear from her eyes and finished taking care of her patients.

Keifer and his other six men did indeed head to town. Keifer sent his men in groups of two. Two would ride in with him from the South end of town, two would circle the town and ride in from the North end of town, and he also positioned two of his men to get on the roofs to cover them from above. He figured he had a fool proof plan. He didn't know who he was up against!

Graham had positioned Andy to a lookout position coming into town. He knew what Keifer looked like. When he saw them coming, he would high tail it over to the Sheriff's Office to let them know. Graham's plan was to make a stand with Ren and Seth in the middle of Main Street. He wanted Andy and Jonah to position themselves behind them as they came down the street.

He had three U.S. Marshall's who had arrived yesterday from the Territorial Office and he then placed them on either side of the street. When he went and got Jonah, Jonah had kissed the surprised Charlie and sent her upstairs to keep her safe. He closed the store and joined his friends.

What he didn't know was that Charlie wasn't about to let anything happen to her friends and all the men who were risking their lives to keep her safe. She ran up the stairs to her bedroom and quickly changed into pants and a shirt. She grabbed her own rifle and fastened on her gun belt just to be on the safe side. She brought up the entire box of bullets she had hidden away and climbed up to the roof of the store. She hid behind the false front that faced Main Street and set herself up ready to handle anything that came up. It was while she waited that she noticed two men running along the roofs of the businesses along the street. That dirty low-down toad sucking piece of scum, Charlie thought! He plans for his men to shoot ours from sitting on top of the buildings like shooting ducks in a gallery. Charlie had other ideas.

Graham waited until Keifer and his two friends were about half way down the street. Andy whistled to him that two more were coming from the opposite end of town. Andy and Jonah waited until they passed and then they came up to them from behind. Mort and Hammerhead, the names of the two thugs, didn't like having guns shoved against their backs and told to drop their weapons. When they hesitated, both Jonah and Andy helped them along by knocking them out with the ends of their rifles. They caught them as they fell so they wouldn't make any noise and alert Keifer that he was going to be two men short. However, the men on the roof saw it all and raised their guns to shoot them. Charlie used two shots, one for each man. As soon as they were shot, they fell off the roofs onto the ground and lay still.

Andy and Jonah looked around as to who was doing the shooting, Jonah saw her first. Charlie gave him a little wave and reloaded her rifle. "Son of a bitch! That girl doesn't do anything that she's told to do when I tell her to do it! She's going to get herself killed!" Jonah cursed in a low voice to Andy.

"Yeah, I agree she's a hell of a woman all right. You do realize that she just saved both of our sorry lives!" Andy argued softly.

"Yes, I do, but I still don't want to take any chances on her life. I want to be the one to wring her neck when all of this is over!" Jonah complained.

Keifer was astonished when he heard two shots ring out. He thought it was his men shooting and watched for one of the Sheriff's and Deputies in front of him to fall down. But instead he saw his own men fall off the roofs, now who in the hell was doing the shooting? It sure wasn't the men in front of him! That's when he turned around and found Andy and Jonah standing with guns pointing at his back. What the hell happened to his other two men?

"That's far enough, Keifer!" Yelled Graham. "Drop your weapons before we open fire on you. I don't need to tell you that there's three men in front of you, two more behind you and another three on the sides of you. You are completely surrounded."

"How do you know who I am? I don't recall ever coming in contact with you before." Keifer asked stalling for time to come up with a way out of this predicament. He knew that he was in one hell of a mess that was for sure!

"Back during the war, when you ran with Quantrill's Raiders, you almost killed several kids. You felt we were worthless, but we survived. We became real soldiers and men. We never forgot how you burned our homes, killed our kin, and tried to kill us too. You don't forget someone you hate so much. I went by the name of Crock back then; Reno and Mac are behind you. Now do you remember?" Graham told him with contempt.

"That was during the war, a lot happens in wartime, surely you don't still hold grudges against me when I was just doing my job?" Keifer asked him, he did indeed remember Crock, Reno, and Mac. All were good with a rifle and with a six-gun. He started sweating, they were indeed in a real jam!

"As a matter of fact, we do still hold grudges against you no matter how long its been, but then two young ladies came to our town and told us about how you operated back in Paducah. Those are the crimes that are going to send you to the Territorial Prison for a very long time and the rest of your men as well."

"Damnit! I knew that Lela and Charlie were here! I want to see those two women! Get them or my men and I won't go quietly, some of you will die just because of two worthless split-tails! They're not worth it, no woman is!" Keifer hollered at them all.

"One of those women just happens to be my wife, Keifer, and I sure don't appreciate you calling her names. Now drop your weapons! All of them, even the knives in your boots and the derringer you carry in your front shirt pocket. You're not getting our women and we'll see you in hell first before we let you kill any of our friends!" Graham responded. He was watching Keifer's eyes for when he would make his first move. He knew this man, he was not going to go quietly. So be it, Graham thought, he'd been wanting to get his hands on him for a very long time.

CHAPTER 18

One of Keifer's men went for his gun, Ren didn't hesitate, and the man fell off his horse with a bullet between his eyes. He had learned early on that if he were called upon to shoot, then he was to shoot to kill. Keifer's other thug was outraged that they had killed his friend, he didn't stop to reason that they were there to kill all of them, he too made the mistake to go for his gun. The Sheriff shot him before he could clear his gun from his holster. He fell with a bullet in his black heart. That left only Keifer.

That's when Bo and his other valley friends came into view with a wagon full of his men. When Keifer realized that he was the only one of his crew left, he slowly raised his arms. He couldn't believe that he had been beaten by a bunch of farmers! He didn't for a moment think that it was over. As long as there was breath in his body, he could still escape. And when he did, he would come back with an even bigger army to burn this town to the ground!

Graham took great delight in stripping Keifer of all his weapons including the ones in his boots and his chest pockets. Keifer had never felt as angry as he watched them take all his weapons away from him. He saw the man called Mac drag two of his men to the jail to lock up with him. Good, he thought, I'll have at least two men helping me escape when I get the chance. But before he was locked up, Graham had other ideas. He swung his fist with all his might and hit Keifer in the mouth, knocking out two teeth in his attack.

"That was for talking trash about my wife you sleaze bag! Now, get up and get in that jail cell! I've spent enough time and energy worrying about you and your men coming into our town and trying to take our women away from us." Graham pushed Keifer away from the door of the cell and locked the door. He was thrilled that they had captured Keifer without any of them being shot or hurt in the process. He couldn't wait to tell Leah that it was over, she was now safe, and they could live their life without worrying about Keifer coming to take out his revenge.

Jonah was having similar thoughts about Charlie. He was going to kiss her until she collapsed against him in surrender and then he was going to strangle her for not doing what she had been told to do! She was safe at last; their little charade was over. They could all go back to living normal lives without worrying about when or even if Keifer would show up and cause trouble.

Charlie met Jonah at the bottom of the stairs and threw herself into his arms. Jonah not only caught her, he proceeded to kiss the breath right out of her. He and Charlie were both shaking by the time he pulled away. "Charlie, so help me God, if you ever pull a stunt like that again after I told you to stay in that room, I'll beat your butt! Do you know how scared I was that a stray bullet could get to you up there on that roof! Those were ruthless men out there, they wouldn't have thought twice about filling you with buckshot whether you were a girl or a boy! Don't ever do anything like that again!" Jonah told her while he still held her close to him.

Charlie pulled a little away from him, "Jonah, I would do it again and again if I knew that I would be helping you stay alive! I don't care if you're yelling at me or even mad at me, I couldn't bear it if something happened to you or one of the others because of trying to keep me safe." She hesitated and then decided to go for broke, "I...love...you...Jonah with all my heart."

Jonah melted at the words she just spoke. He looked at Charlie and whispered back at her, "And I...love...you, Charlie, even though you are the biggest pain in the ass I've ever met! I don't know how I'm going to live with you for the rest of our lives without wringing your neck at least once a week." He hesitated, and then asked, "Charlie would you do me the very great honor of marrying me and making my life hell for the next thirty or forty years?" Jonah loved Charlie without any rhyme or reason, he just knew that without her his life would be worth nothing.

"Oh, Jonah, I would love to marry you! I can't imagine not having you around always telling me what to do! I also promise to make your life hell at least once a week just to keep you happy, how is that?" Charlie giggled as he kissed her again.

"Sounds like heaven, honey!" Jonah hugged her and then told her to go up and change in to one of her own clothes and to fix her hair the way she liked to fix it, her hiding days were over. He wanted the whole town to see his bride as the beautiful young woman she really was. Charlie gave a little squeal and ran up the stairs. Jonah went to reopen up his store.

Meanwhile, Graham was busy kissing the tears from Leah's face. She was so relieved that he was safe and that no one had gotten hurt keeping her and Charlie safe. "It's over sweetheart, we can live our lives without worrying when and if Keifer will show up. He's locked up in our jail and won't be going anywhere except the Territorial Prison after the Circuit Judge comes and tries him and his men. You're free, my Leah, to be you again. No more pillows or ugly hats and glasses to wear. I want the whole town to see my beautiful bride and wife." He turned to Annalise and Andy, "I'm going to take my wife home to change into her real clothes, and then I'll bring her back to finish out the day. Maybe by then her hands will stop shaking so she can sew. Thanks, Andy for all your help in keeping her safe." He paused, "I'm sorry that we didn't tell you everything at the very start, Annalise, but the fewer people that knew about Charlie and Leah the better we had of keeping it a secret. Besides that, you had a baby to deliver and a shop to run, not to mention that you are married to Andy, you have to keep him in line, too!"

"No explanations are necessary, Graham. I'm just glad I won't lose the best seamstress in the territory! Go home, Leah, everything will still be here when you return." Annalise and Andy shooed them out the door. The two went home happily.

Getting out of her costume and putting on her real clothes was a joy. Especially with Graham helping her, of course he wanted to make love to her before he took her back to Annalise and nothing could make her happier than to love him back. It was a glowing Leah that went back to work that afternoon. Graham kissed her good bye at the door and whistled all the way back to the jail.

Bo and his friends had unloaded the six bodies and also helped carry the four additional bodies of Keifer's men to the undertaker. They shook hands with Graham, Ren, and Seth and agreed that it was a successful day all things considered. Bo told them to call if they needed their help in the future, and they left for the valley.

The town couldn't believe the change in Lottie/Charlie and Leah/Lela. How could two such beautiful women have been in their town and they didn't even know it? They were thrilled that Graham and Jonah had found love and to welcome the two ladies to Trinity. They even understood why they had changed their names and their appearances to deceive them. It had been to keep them alive and safe, that was enough of a reason out here in the wild territory where everyone struggled to stay alive and survive.

The U.S. Marshalls wired for more men to take Keifer and his two men back to stand trial in Billings. They didn't want to take the chance of them getting away and wreaking havoc again on this little town.

CHAPTER 19

It was a very happy day for Lela and Charlie. They had both found love and were forever removed from the shadow of Keifer and his men. Their future looked very bright. The two couples ate dinner at the Crocker's that night. Charlie was so happy to be able to get out of the store and her rooms above the store for the first time in many months. The men were very much in love with their women and their women were in awe over their chosen husbands. The two couples spent several hours talking over all the changes that would be made now that Keifer was locked up safe and sound.

Charlie wanted to go visit her mother and her sisters. She had missed them more than she ever thought possible. She also wanted Jonah to ask her mother for her hand in marriage. She wanted to marry him as soon as possible before he changed his mind! Jonah assured her he wasn't going to change his mind in the next thirty or forty years, and he looked forward to meeting the rest of Charlie's family. He wondered if her two sisters were anything like Charlie was, heaven help the young men that fell in love with them! They were sure to lead them a merry chase. He wanted to marry Charlie as soon as possible, too, but it was because he was having serious trouble keeping his hands off his future wife. Jonah's body responded to her kisses and hugs all too well, he couldn't wait to make her his in body and soul.

It was late when Jonah and Charlie finally left to go home. Graham and Lela went to bed and made love far into the night. It was the perfect way to end every day.

Morning brought a first for Trinity, Jonah closed the Mercantile and rented a buggy and horse to take Charlie home to see her family. They had a wonderful ride out to the valley talking all about the wedding that Charlie hoped they would have in the next few days. It had been a few years since Jonah had traveled out to the valley and he was impressed at all the changes that the men and their wives had made to their land.

Their cabins were built very sturdy to last for generations. Crops were growing at an alarming rate, the corn already reaching to a man's shoulders and the wheat blowing almost thigh high in the wind. He could see what looked like hundreds of cattle grazing on the lush grass and cattle, oxen, mules and horses grazing side by side. Cords of wood were stacked by each of the cabins, and from the smell of smoked meat, their smoke houses were filled with game. Large gardens were situated by each of the homes, as well as, a barn and corrals. Besides each of the cabins, flowers bloomed and carried a heady aroma to all who passed by. Clothes lines were filled with clean clothes and diapers drying in the gentle wind. He saw several women churning butter outside on the porch watching children play in the yard or on blankets that lay in the grass. It looked so peaceful and serene, it almost took your breath away.

Jonah was surprised that Charlie's mother looked so young to have three such beautiful daughters. The sight of Charlie and her two sisters was enough to make you look once and then again to make sure you weren't seeing a fanciful vision instead of three magnificent young ladies. They hugged and kissed each other as if Charlie had been gone for years instead of just a few months! It was several minutes before Charlie got around to introducing Jonah to her family. And then she pulled him up beside her smiling, "Mama, Dani, and Jo, I want to introduce Jonah McDonald, my fiancé! He wants to marry me, and I love him so much, I want to marry him, too!"

Amid many squeals of delight from her sisters, Jonah shook Willa's hand. "Mrs. Bellamy, I would like to officially ask for Charlie's hand in marriage. I love her very much, and although she drives me crazy much of the time I'm with her, I can't imagine life without her. I promise to love her, provide for her and any children we might have, protect her with my life, and to try to keep her in line. As much as I might threaten, I will never raise a hand in anger to her or see her hurt in any way. Would you agree to let me marry Charlie?"

"Mr. McDonald, it sounds like you know my daughter very well indeed, and if after knowing her and knowing all the trouble she can get into, you still want to marry her, I give you my blessing and that of her father. He wanted nothing more than to see all of his children settled with good men. I think Charlie's found a very good man in you. Welcome to the family!" Willa told a grinning Jonah and then gave him a hug and kiss on the cheek. "It looks like we have a wedding to plan! Will you join us for lunch, and we can talk?"

Jonah put his arm around Charlie and together they walked into the cabin with her mother and two sisters. None of them felt they could be happier or prouder of the little family.

A simple wedding was planned. They were going to be married there in the valley with all their friends and family invited to attend the happy event in two weeks. Willa would give Charlie away, and Dani and Jo would be her bridesmaids. Jonah was going to ask Andy and Graham to stand up for him. He planned on sending a wire to Father Callahan to come and officiate the wedding. Willa and her girls went into high gear making a wedding dress for Charlie and making two new dresses for Dani and Jo. The rest of the valley got into the act to help the happy couple. A steer would be roasted Texas style over a pit and cooked until it was tender. Each of the women in the valley was going to make a pot of mashed potatoes and a pot of a vegetable, some corn, some green beans, or some beets. Willa and her girls would be making bread for the entire reception. Not to be left out, Lela and Annalise asked to make and bring out the wedding cake. It was going to be a celebration that none of them would soon forget!

Willa made Charlie a soft white dress of eyelet, lined with satin. It was simply made with a flowing skirt that made her waist appear very small and showed off her perfect figure. She even made her a veil that hung down to her waist along with her beautiful hair. Dani and Jo were dressed in similar gowns, but they were made of a bright blue that brought out the color of their eyes and shone up brightly against the red of Dani's hair and the platinum white hair of Jo. Willa planned to wear her favorite Sunday go to church dress. It was long-sleeved with lace around the end of both sleeves and around the Mandarin collar as well. It was in a pale grey silk and it was the very last dress that Ed had bought for her before he died. By wearing the dress, Willa felt that Ed would be there with her giving their daughter away at her marriage.

On the day of the wedding, Jo and Dani went out into the woods and collected every flower they could find and brought them back to decorate the tables, porch, and for Charlie to carry. Tables were set up and benches were brought out so that there was room for everyone in the valley and from town to sit and enjoy the day. Unbeknown to the happy couple, Andy and Graham had arranged for a few fellows from town to bring their fiddles so they could dance after the service was finished. It promised to be a wonderful wedding. Red was hoping that he would have the chance of dancing with Dani before the day was over and holding her in his arms. Mason was even giving the idea of dancing with Jo some thought. She wasn't so bad for a girl, he thought.

Father Callahan had arrived the day before and stayed with Molly, Bo, and their boys. Wolf and the rest of the Sioux warriors had left to go back home. They promised to return in the coming months before they went north for the winter. Boone went with them. He was fully healed and had loved being spoiled by Molly. He had critters to hunt and skins to accumulate to be able to buy the supplies he needed for the winter months. He bid good bye to the only family he had ever had. Wolf had bid a sorrowful good bye to Jo in the woods and had given her a kiss, her first. He vowed to come back often to see her and wait for her to grow up. Skah promised to wait until Wolf came back. She was going to miss running through the woods with him every day. But she also knew that she was only twelve years old, too young to be married even to Wolf.

Every single one of the men and women in the valley were dressed in their very best clothes. It wasn't every day that they could stop working and watch one of their own get married and spend the day talking to their friends.

Charlie took their breath away when she walked down the steps with Willa to meet a very nervous groom in Jonah. He couldn't wait to make her his. Father Callahan gave a lovely ceremony and when he announced that Jonah could now kiss the bride, Jonah didn't waste any time doing just that! Just as the party had started to get under way, Violet Greer's water broke!

Molly gave the boys to Bo and Father Callahan, asked May and Miller to watch over Henry Lee and Thomas, Vi's two older boys, and then climbed into the Greer's wagon to deliver her baby. Molly had Sam stop at her home to get her medical bag, some newspapers she had accumulated, and an oilcloth to cover the bed with. By the time they arrived at the Greer's cabin, Violet was having some rather strong contractions. Molly had Sam help Vi out of her wet clothes and then to help her take a bath while she remade the bed with the oilcloth and newspapers and a clean sheet. By the time Sam carried Vi to the bed, Vi was having contraction after contraction, and she barely had time to rest between them. Molly examined Vi and told her that this delivery was not very far away. Vi just smiled and hung onto Sam's strong hands.

Molly went to heat up some water to sterilize the string and scissors she would use to cut the cord and tie it off. Everything was going so fast, she wished she had several more hands to get everything done in time. Suddenly Ethel was there. She had left the party and Lizzy with Calvin to help her friend deliver this baby. Molly was so relieved she almost cried.

In no time Molly positioned herself at the foot of their bed. "Vi, I can see the head crowning. When you feel like pushing, push. Everything is ready for this baby to be born. I know how much you wanted another baby. I promise that this one will never be taken from you and sold."

Vi pushed with tears running down her face and the baby slipped into Molly's waiting hands. In seconds, Molly had the mucus cleared from the baby's mouth and the cord cut, baby Greer was crying angrily much to the joy of everyone in the room. Ethel took the baby and started washing it, and Molly took over with Vi getting the afterbirth out by massaging her stomach. They still hadn't announced the sex of the baby.

"Oh, Vi! You have a beautiful little girl! I'm so happy that my little Lizzy will have friends to play with!" Ethel told Vi and Sam who were beaming.

"Hear that, honey! We got a little girl at last! I figured that we'd have another boy, but with already having two sons in Henry Lee and Thomas, I knew how much you wanted a girl. God's been very good to us!" Sam told her kissing her and going to look over his new daughter.

Rolling up the bloody newspapers, Molly put them aside and then washed the tired limbs of Violet and put her in a clean nightgown. Then she checked out the little baby. It was perfect, Molly thought she would be as beautiful as her mother when she grew up. She put the little bundle into the waiting hands of her mother. "Well, what are you going to name her?" Molly asked as she continued to clean up from the birth.

"My mama named me after a flower, I think we'll continue the tradition. We're going to call her Lillian, Lilly for short. Is that all right with you, Sam?" Violet asked her husband.

"I'd say it's perfect. Do you think that Father Callahan will baptize her and Faith before he heads back to Billings?" Sam inquired, his eyes not leaving his wife or daughter for an instant.

"I'm sure he would be honored. I'll ask him when Ethel and I go back to the party. Just let us clean up here and put on some dinner for you eat. We'll bring the boys back in a few hours, that way you'll have time to take a rest before they get here. I will arrange with the other women to have one of us come over here every day until you're up on your feet again. I know that you have vegetables to can and Sam has fields to harvest, but we'll see that it all gets done. Congratulations on a beautiful little girl!" Molly kissed the new baby and Vi on the forehead.

"Thank you, Molly, for helping us deliver our baby. And for all the help from each of the ladies in the valley. I just feel so blessed to live here where my children will never know the sting of a whip on their backs or to be taken from me and Sam." Vi spoke quietly into the room even as she fell asleep. Sam took his daughter and put her into her cradle and covered her with a little quilt that Vi had made. Then he helped the two women clean up the room and take the soiled cloth and newspapers outside.

245

While Molly started up pot of vegetable soup, Ethel washed out the sheets and nightgowns and hung them on the line. Sam burned the newspapers and began his chores while the women were still here, that way when they left, he would be in the cabin to help Vi in whatever needed done. He was a very happy man.

By the time that Molly and Ethel got back to the party, it was drawing to a close. Everyone was thrilled that all went well with Violet, and each woman chose a day to go over and help her out. Charlie and Jonah were getting ready to head back to town with the Renosso's and the Crocker's. Charlie promised to visit soon with her family. The women of the valley gave Charlie and Jonah a new quilt for their bed in a beautiful wedding ring pattern. Charlie was thrilled and blushed thinking of her wedding night with Jonah.

The three couples left, and the rest of the valley loaded up the tables and benches and headed for home. Willa was grateful for all their help in cleaning up and making them feel like part of the valley of friends. That night as she prepared for bed, she prayed to God and talked to Ed. "God, thank you for getting us safely to this wonderful valley and meeting all these friends. Thank you for giving my Charlie a good man to love and care for her. I ask you to continue to bless my family and friends... Ed, I know you were watching over Charlie and the rest of us. You'd like Jonah, he knows our daughter well enough to love her despite her many flaws. Your wish for Charlie to be happy came true. I

246

love you Ed and miss you every day, but I know you're still with us and watching over us...Amen. "Then Willa lay down and almost fell instantly asleep. She was happy and content, and for now that was enough.

CHAPTER 20

Charlie's wedding night with Jonah was perfect as far as Charlie and Jonah were concerned. Never had a groom been so gentle in loving his wife on their first of many nights together. Charlie had stars in her eyes when they woke up together. They both walked around on a cloud until the sheriff's office received a telegram from the U.S. Marshall's that Keifer and his two men had broken loose and killed several of the Marshalls in their bid for freedom.

Charlie and Lela knew in their hearts that Keifer was headed back to Trinity to avenge his being taken into custody. Neither wanted anything to happen to their men or anyone else in the valley or town. Graham, Ren, and Seth with Jonah and Andy sat down to settle on the best way to keep everyone safe when they showed up again. Graham knew in his heart that this time they wouldn't be as lucky as the first time without anyone getting injured. But he would never give up Leah/Lela unless he were dead, and he saw the grim look on Jonah's face and knew he felt the same about Charlie/Lottie.

Last time they had kept the fact that wanted men were coming to Trinity a secret from the town, this time they let every man, woman, business, and rancher or farmer know what was coming their way. Many knew of Quantrill's Raiders and how ruthless they were during the War Between the States. Lookouts were posted in town and in the valley. They would not go down easily.

Ren was sent out to warn the valley of Keifer's escape and the possibility of him coming back to Trinity to wreck vengeance on the ones who had captured him in the first place. Bo and Tate had started thrashing wheat in the valley, but they agreed to meet tonight after dinner and their chores were done. Safety for all of them came first. Ren spread the word to the rest of the ranchers and then headed back to town. They had their own meeting to take care of and to find a way to keep the inhabitants safe. In the back of Ren's mind, was the threat of Keifer's to burn the entire town down to get what he wanted. Ren was determined that was not going to happen.

Lela liked being called Leah instead of Lela. She felt like she had started over here in Trinity, and a new beginning meant a new name. Plus, there was the fact that Annalise and Andy had named little Annaleigh after Leah not Lela. Graham didn't care what she was called, she was his woman no matter what. Leah thought that it would be a good thing if the women of Trinity came to a meeting to warn them about the threat coming to their little town. They might be the deciding factor in keeping them all safe and sound. Graham and Seth agreed. Word was sent from house to house that a meeting would be held tonight in the church to talk about a very real threat coming to Trinity.

At 7:00 o'clock, the church was crammed with almost everyone that could walk in town. Seth took over the meeting telling them about Keifer Kutter and everything he was accused of doing with Quantrill's Raiders in the War Between the States. He told them he was on the way to Trinity to get vengeance on the town that had captured him and two of his men. Graham told the town that he had already been there once before and he had brought a dozen of his thugs with him, only two survived the outcome. This time he felt that he would bring even more, and they wanted no harm to come to any of them.

Lookouts would be posted outside of town from the north and from the south. They would have men patrolling the streets and checking out every business in town daily and nightly. Men would be armed taking their families to the store, to the church, to school, or any other errand they had to carry out. Women were urged to keep a close eye on their children and when the signal was given to take them to a safe place to hide. Those women who could shoot, were urged to carry a rifle or derringer with them at all times. Remembering that Kutter had sent men up on the roofs before, men were sent to the roofs to watch over the town as well. In addition to the extra precautions, they also made a fire wall around the entire town just in case Keifer chose to carry out his threat of burning them out. They hoped they had every contingency covered. Now all they had left to do was wait and pray.

Similar actions were being taken by the men in the valley. Firewalls were dug around every homestead in the valley. The men didn't want to lose their crops, but they were a minor worry considering they might be giving up their lives instead of a corn crop or a wheat crop. Women practiced target practice every day. No one walked around without a gun on them. They even took them to the outhouse with them! They were determined that they would not let Keifer or his men win.

Keifer arrived on the outskirts of Trinity three days later. The last time he came to get the two women, he had split his men, half of his men rode on the valley and the other half rode with him into town. This time would be different. They would all ride together on the town, and then after they were victorious, they would ride on the valley and wipe out the settlers that had defeated them last time. He would be damned if he would let his men be beaten by a bunch of farmers!

Keifer's men rode in swiftly shooting at anything that moved. Graham had been right, last time he came with a dozen men, this time he had over twenty riding with him. With that much fire power, he didn't think that it would take too long to get control of the entire town. And that was the problem, he didn't think or give the men and women of Trinity much credit for preparing for them.

Keifer's men were shooting and just as quickly shots were fired at them from the rooftops and from the doorways. Riding down the middle of the streets didn't give them that much cover to keep from getting shot, thick heavy wooden doors helped protect them from the hundreds of bullets that were flying every which way. One by one Keifer's men started falling, but they weren't getting up. A few tried to hide behind water troughs, but with men returning fire from all directions, that idea didn't work out very well.

Keifer watched as his men fell and his frustration grew. By God, he'd told them he'd burn them out, he'd do just that! He sounded the order to retreat and he and his men started a fire to burn down the entire town. Only the fire hit the firewall of freshly dug dirt and came back towards them! After fighting the fire, he decided to ride toward the valley and burn them out instead and capture them as they ran for safety. The valley was ready for them.

The fire wall the valley had set up defeated Keifer's attempts to burn them out, too. He was fit to be tied! How could a bunch of clods outwit him??! He didn't know which ranch belonged to whom, he just chose one at random. He made the mistake of choosing Bo Callahan's. Inside the home, they had Bo, Molly, and Rusty. In the loft, they had Boone and Wolf. As they circled the cabin and began firing on them, Bo and his friends fired back. Several of Keifer's men fell before Bo's friends came up and started firing from all sides.

Keifer and his men never had a chance. Within minutes, not a man was standing. Calvin and Sam started rounding up the horses and putting them in Bo's corral. Tate and Miller started loading up bodies into Bo's wagon. Rusty and Red tied up any and all remaining men. Molly was busy tying up wounds to keep them alive to be delivered to the Trinity jail. No one noticed that Keifer was slowly pulling down his arm to his back to pull up another weapon. He didn't care who he killed but he wasn't going to go back to prison. He pulled up his gun and set his sights on Molly. If he killed their women it would hurt them even more. The only one who noticed his movement was Red Dalton, he dived in front of Molly just as Keifer fired. He took the bullet meant for her, but before he fell, he emptied his gun into Keifer's body. It jerked as each bullet found its mark. Red fell to the ground. Molly rushed over. She had seen him give his life to save hers, she would be forever grateful that she would live to see her two boys grow up.

"Bo, help me get Red into the cabin! I've got to save him, he jumped in front of the bullet that Keifer had meant for me!" Molly was crying even as she was trying to stop the flow of blood from his body.

Red smiled at the pretty little redhead that had made his friend Bo so happy, "Don't worry...Molly...I made it through the war...with little to show for all my efforts. Me and Rusty plan on living here in this beautiful valley of ours forever...I'm not ever wanting to leave it...Looks

like I'm going to get my wish to stay here forever..."
Red closed his eyes as it got harder and harder to talk.
"I'll be watching over all of you..."

Molly cried even harder and worked quickly and
efficiently to get the bleeding stopped. But she was
fighting a losing battle. Red's life's blood slipped
through her fingers and he died. Molly cried as if her
heart was broken, and Bo held her in his arms. He
couldn't believe that Red would no longer be a part of
their little family, he was so young to die and all too
soon he was gone. He remembered too many times that
they had fought together in the war, they had laughed as
something silly they had seen, or they had talked about
what they wanted when the war was finally over. Red
had wanted peace and to live in a land that planted
seeds in the ground, not young broken bodies that had
died way too soon.

CHAPTER 21

When they brought the bodies into town, Bo and Tate told them about Red's jumping in front of the bullet meant for Molly, Bo's wife. They hated to see the shock and misery reflected on their faces.

Trinity buried the last of Keifer's men and Keifer in the graveyard on the outskirts of town. The citizens were thrilled that they had stood together to with stand the ruthless killers, and that their little town was still there.

They buried Red in the little graveyard in the valley. This was where May and Miller had buried their daughter, April. This is where Willa buried her husband, Ed. This is where Rusty buried his friend and adopted son. It was a beautiful place to stay for all eternity.

Trinity and the valley flourished. The good people of Trinity had become friends during the danger of Keifer and his men. Charlie and Jonah, and Graham and Leah became even closer. Andy and Annalise joined their families with their own. The three couples were often seen going to each other's houses for dinner. By Christmas, both Charlie and Leah could announce that they were each pregnant and due sometime in the summer. Ren was spending more and more time with

Dani, Rusty and Willa enjoyed each other's company and talked about making it permanent one of these days, and Jo wrote to Wolf often of her thoughts and prayers for his safe return. Life went on in the valley and in Trinity. Time is an excellent healer of hearts, the people of the Yellowstone valley had many blessings and few regrets.

The End

Note from the Author

I want to personally thank you for your time and effort in the reading of this book. I love writing, and I owe it to my readers to do the best I can. The best source of input to influence my future efforts is your feedback. Please take just a few minutes to share whatever thoughts you may have on this book by going to https://www.amazon.com/author/m_dipaolo and submit a rating and, if you wish, some comments as well. I would really appreciate it.

ABOUT THE AUTHOR

Marcella (Marky) DiPaolo was raised as a farm girl in Moro, Illinois. She was one of six children, and they all interacted daily with their loving parents and grandparents who served as ideal role models for them as they grew up on the farm. Upon graduating from high school, Marcella started her career in business. She also went to college, initially to become an accountant. It was in the business world that she met the person with whom she wanted to share the rest of her life.

It didn't take long for the young couple to start filling up their home with children. It was in the raising of her own that she realized that working with kids was her passion. She decided that teaching was the direction she wanted to go. During the early years, she was the one that stayed home to watch the kids while her husband worked during the day and went to school at night to complete his education. Once finished, he spent his evenings with the children, so she could go on and complete her BA in Elementary Education and later getting a Masters with a concentration in mathematics.

After more than thirty-five years of teaching, she recently retired but continues to teach from time to time as a substitute at a local parochial school. Over the years, Mrs. D., as she is referred to by her students, was recognized for her teaching accomplishments having received several awards and other forms of recognition. 'Mrs. D' has certainly had a very special effect on a lot of young people, all of whom she still considers members of her 'extended' family.

Marcella has a lot of other interests as well. In addition to a voracious appetite for romantic plots and characters, she is also fond of adventure stories and mysteries. She also loves to watch sports, play golf, eat chocolate, and spend as much time as possible with her family.

Marcella's love of reading began at a very early age. However, she never dreamed she might become a writer until much later in life. Being somewhat addicted to historical romances, both in books and on the screen, she has been exposed to a lot of writing styles. This experience and her time on the farm, raising a family, and all those years in the classroom have provided her with a wealth of ideas to apply to her writing career.

Books Written by Marcella DiPaolo

Clear Water Bride Series
    Bargain Bride
    Troubled Bride
    Forgotten Bride
    Reluctant Bride
    Runaway Bride
Morgan Brothers Storm Series
    Above the Storm
    After the Storm
    Beyond the Storm
Pine City Chance Series
    Taking a Chance
    A Second Chance
Trinity Series
    The Escape to Trinity
    The Refuge in Trinity
    The Hope of Trinity
Others (Not Part of a Series)
    Promises to Keep
    Heart to Heart

Made in the USA
Columbia, SC
09 June 2024